Ariadne's Crown

By: Meadoe Hora

For my boys. Always.

SHIP 1

Wearing my plain *white* tunic, I blended in. I breathed the fresh air, felt the sunshine bounce off my face and let it wash over me. Freedom. I slouched my shoulders in defiance of nobody because there was nobody to tell me to walk straight. In fact, nobody paid any attention to me. I was just a girl at the market. I could be anybody. Here, there were serving girls and wives, bustling about haggling over food for the day or trinkets or clothing. Like me, they knew what was expected of them and they did it without question. Unlike me, they didn't have to sneak out to get here.

In the marketplace, the world spread out over blankets haphazardly forming rows. Some, shielded by the sun with hastily built shelters while others baked in the sun. Spices from exotic locations delivered by sailors who collected stories like scars perfumed the air. Their scent mingled with freshly baked bread and food of all kinds. I breathed it all in, the riot of smells. As I walked, an artist called out to me to purchase his pottery, but I kept walking. I loved how the voices of the village mingled together in a tapestry.

"Scarab right from Egypt…"

"Finest copper headpiece to match your beauty…"

"Fresh today…"

A group of giggling kids ran past me, in the middle of some game with rules known only to them. My eye caught the sparkle of jewelry glinting in the sunlight. I picked up a sleek, intricately carved bronze bracelet and then discarded it, thinking its beauty was better suited to my sister, Phaedre. The sweet smell of fresh bread pulled me along to the far end of the market. On a blanket, baskets piled high with loaves of bread, honey cakes and sweet figs tempted me. Three women stood gossiping in a tight circle, with the tall, craggy woman holding court.

I don't remember the first time I heard my mother whispered about or the words "white bull" snickered behind cupped hands. Usually, I brushed it off. However, there was something about the woman's superior tone and the judgmental arch of her eyebrow that annoyed me. Like a fussy peacock, she leaned

7

into her younger friend.

"My father was there at the festival when the king didn't sacrifice his precious white bull." She nodded, accentuating the *white bull* like it was a curse word.

"Talked about it all the time. That thing was the biggest bull he had ever seen, all white, with red eyes and giant horns. The king just couldn't give it up, but you can't fool the gods. They always get theirs. After that, the harvest was the worst in years. When the earth under your feet moves, you take notice." She cackled at her own joke and poked the younger woman in the ribs with her elbow.

"Everyone made offerings to make the gods happy again. My father sacrificed our fattest sheep, while that white bull walked free. Our fattest sheep." She paused, making sure she still had their attention and then gestured towards the palace and raised an eyebrow at the younger woman. "The queen just mooned for that white bull, always following it around and bringing it food. Everyone said she was cursed." None of them even noticed I was standing there. My hands clenched.

"Cursed is right," her older friend added. "I sure wouldn't send my daughter to work there. No matter how much coin it's worth."

The younger one shrank back and then shook her head. "Well, all I know is," she replied, shifting her basket to the other hip. "After I got here, my son was so sick. I didn't know what to do. I didn't know anyone. So, I took him to the palace. The queen-she didn't turn me away. She was kind. She mixed up a poultice for his chest and gave me some herbs for tea. After that, he recovered. Thank the gods." She kissed her fingertips and sent it up to the sky.

I smiled. To me, my mother was many things, cold and beautiful. She wasn't defined by a slanderous story, but by her healing hands. Although she could be hard, I have seen her mix the herbs to cure the plague and apply them herself to the sick sons of the shepherd.

The first woman snorted in amusement. She straightened her back and looked over the top of her long nose and scoffed. "Well, I'm glad for your boy, but mark my words. There's darkness in that palace. I wouldn't take her herbs if my life depended on it." She preened and my blood rose. I glared at her. With a start, I realized I recognized this horrible woman putting on airs. She was the fisherman's wife.

Before I could stop myself, I was speaking. "Really?" I said, picking up a parcel of honey cakes. "Is that why you were at the palace begging for something to keep your husband in your bed?" I widened my eyes in innocence and held out a coin. Nobody took it. All three woman stared back at me, mouths open. Nobody moved. The fisherman's wife turned a purple shade of red and clenched her fist.

"What's the meaning of these lies, girl?" she demanded. I didn't respond, but I couldn't help a

9

little grin from slipping out. I saw the recognition on her face. We both knew what I said was true. She pulled a spoon out of a basket of grain and raised it. "Girl, if you don't get out of here, I'm going to teach you some manners." She smacked her hand with the large spoon for emphasis. I shrugged my shoulders, grabbed another honey cake and ran.

"Stop that thief," one of them yelled as I disappeared into the market.

I ran through the sellers, jumping over blankets until I arrived giggly and breathless at the other end of the market. Nobody made a move to stop me. After the initial commotion, even that hateful woman gave up and stopped yelling. I should have felt guilty. If my mother had heard what I said, she would have punished me. She was like that. No matter what people said, it didn't bother her. She was always in control, always two moves ahead. My inability to hide my feelings disappointed her, along with my unruly hair which never stayed in place. I could feel now that it had broken out of its clip and reached up to tuck it back into place.

I was at the far corner of the market, where the slaves were traded. Here, there was no happy chatter or friendly bartering. Instead of spices, bread and food, the rank smell of unwashed bodies and fear lingered in the air. When I came with Thalia, my maid, we avoided this corner of the market. Thalia wouldn't come near it. Even now, I stayed a safe distance, but I could see the block was full – mostly women with empty eyes, some shielding children with their bodies. There were a few men, but not many. Nobody made eye contact- everybody looked up or down.

I caught the glance of a young girl of about five years old fidgeting in front of her mother and was surprised when she didn't look away. Already, she had seen too much of the world, but her eyes were still soft. I felt myself pulled toward her, like we were connected on a string that kept getting shorter until I stood right in front of her. Without the shorn cut of a slave, she would probably not look any different from the children running and laughing through the palace. The uncomfortable thought struck me that had the wars of our island turned out differently, it could be Phaedre and me on that block. I wished I could take the girl with me – away from the block and these people. Let her hair flow free and her smile return.

I held out the honey cake and smiled, but she didn't move. Her eyes widened, locked in on the cake. Just then, a hulking man came out from behind the block. He wore fine clothes, but they were dirty and his face was contorted in anger.

"Hey! What are you doing? Get away from her," he yelled. Thumping the handle of a whip on his open hand, he rolled his eyes over me. For a moment, I thought of taking her hand and pulling her off the block, running together to safety. He lunged toward me and I snapped out of it. I lacked the power to protect anyone. I was not a warrior or an Amazon - just a girl who wasn't supposed to be here. I took off running as fast as I could, back to the safety of the crowd. He didn't follow. I whispered a brief prayer to Hera for the girl and hurried back to the palace, my heart thumping.

I headed straight for my quarters in the women's area to find Thalia, my maid, and get cleaned up. Thalia looked up from straightening the room and frowned.

"You're late!" she scolded. "They're already gathered to work on the tapestry."

Quickly, she helped me out of my plain tunic and back into my green chiton with the delicate pleats that shimmered in the light. She let my hair down and wrestled it into place to secure it with a headband. As she worked, I told her about what I said to the fisherman's wife, but not about the slave trader. Her eyes lit up at the honey cake in my hand. When Thalia was finished, I once again looked like a shiny version of myself and I shed the bearing of a girl with time to wander and hurried off to find my mother and sister in the weaving room.

My mother stood at the loom, which rested upright against the wall with the tapestry rolled up at the top and weights swinging at the bottom. After months of working on it, this tapestry was coming together nicely. The pattern of olive branches and laurel leaves worked their way through and around the bull, the symbol of my father's power. He would be pleased. The shades of green blended together to create a texture and a softness that contrasted sharply with the powerful bull. My mother weaved by hand, rhythmically passing the thread over and under the warp threads, which strung from top to bottom to form the base. My sister, Phaedre, sat at her feet, with her spindle and distaff, turning the wool into thread. Neither looked up when I entered the room.

"Ariadne, you were not in your quarters when Phaedre came to collect you," my mother said coolly, looking up over her weaving to take in my appearance.

By reflex, I smoothed my hair. "Sorry, Mother," I replied quickly, bowing my head. "I was checking on some matters for dinner tonight. I came right here when I realized the hour."

We both knew I was lying. She studied my face, deciding whether or not she was going to pursue it, furrowed her brow and nodded, motioning to the basket of raw wool. "Please start on that. I believe we will need some more white for the bull."

From her stool, Phaedre rolled her eyes. I took out my spindle and distaff, which was a long rod to collect the thread. The basket of wool looked fresh. Perhaps this is what Thalia had been working on this morning. Before the wool was ready for spinning, it had to be worked through, washed and brushed. That job was not suitable for ladies and thus was delegated to the servants. Holding the distaff upright, I got to work rolling the wool on my leg, making it twist into a rough thread and then fed it to the spindle. I gave the spindle a twirl and dropped it, keeping my eye on it as it spun. Over and again, I fed the fibers gently into the developing strand. As the thread formed, the market faded in my memory and I concentrated on the task in front of me.

The challenge is to keep it even to get a long, smooth thread. That part was difficult to learn and I remember many hours spent at my nurse, Alcina's feet trying to master it. Phaedre, always happy to be the star student, glowed when she picked it up much quicker than me. Even now, she spins like Athena, as if the spindle was an extension of her arm.

It was nice to sit with my sister and mother in companionable silence, but the air was starting to feel heavy. Phaedre broke the silence with a song of love and sorrow. It was one of our favorites from when we were younger. The song tells the story of Demeter and her daughter, Persephone, and the changing of the seasons. As she sang, the spindles swirled and wool turned into thread. My mother wove in silence.

Demeter was a Goddess of the harvest. Her beautiful daughter, Persephone, was her pride. Persephone had a natural beauty with a carefree spirit that couldn't help but draw attention. One day, Persephone got distracted by a Narcissus flower and

14

strayed too far from her mother's protective reach. Some say she was lured away. The poets can never agree on the details. Anyway, the ground opened up and Hades, God of the Underworld, appeared in all his dark power. Enamored with her, Hades swept her away to the underworld in a chariot of darkness pulled by black horses. I always wondered if she was scared or if she was so in love with Hades that she didn't notice the death all around her.

Phaedre's clear, lilting voice rose with tension as she sang of Demeter, wild with grief, scouring the country for her lost daughter. We stole glances at our mother, whose back was rigid, her face concentrating on her weave, seemingly unaware and unconcerned about the despair caused by a lost daughter.

Without Demeter's attentions, the lush farmland shriveled and died. It got so bad that Zeus feared there would be famine and he sent Hermes, the messenger god, to the underworld to negotiate with Hades. Instead of a scared, silly girl enamored by her reflection or a pretty trinket, he found Persephone a beautiful goddess of the underworld, radiant and mysterious. She was happy. Although Hades loved her, he knew he had to obey Zeus. So, he agreed to let Persephone visit her mother, on the condition that she return to him every year. Each year, Demeter watches her daughter die to return to the Underworld. In her sorrow, nothing grows and the fields lie barren. Each spring, Persephone is reborn, arriving on a path of flowers. Demeter's joy wakes up the earth, bringing spring and abundance.

Phaedre's song ended with the promise of hope. We exchanged glances and stifled a giggle. When we were younger, we would coo about how romantic it was, how handsome Hades must have been – all dark and mysterious and how their love forever changed the world.

"Stupid girl," my mother said. "She should have fled the moment she saw that black chariot. Nothing good comes from being loved by a god."

* * *

It started as a dot in the distance, a piece of sky broken on the horizon. From my rock in the outcropping, I watched the ship edge closer. Neither of us was supposed to be here. It was my day for sewing, but I hated sewing. So, when I thought I wouldn't be missed, I slipped out to enjoy the golden sunshine of spring. Somehow, I always ended up at the sea.

When I was small, my nurse, Alcina, and I would go to the bluff and look out over the sea. The wind whipped our hair and threw our tunics. Alcina held my hand tight to keep me safe. I held hers to keep her next to me. She told me stories of the beginning of the world, how the Titans fell to the Olympians and all of their squabbles, but my favorite stories were of her home across the sea. Did they play the same games us us? Eat the same food? What did the sea look like from their shores? Over and over, I asked her to tell me stories of Athens. Alcina was the first to see the wander in my eyes, the way I looked out over the horizon where the sky melted into the water, wondering what was out there. From the bluff, we could see all of the ports up the coast and watch all the ships coming and going. I wondered where they went and what marvels they saw as their sails faded out of sight over the horizon. Alcina told me of the six-headed Scylla, who laid in wait for sailors in the straights and the beautiful Sirens whose songs led sailors to their deaths. The sea was wild and free and dangerous. It was a promise. The opposite of our life in the palace. When it was time to return, we would smooth our tunics, carefully replace the stray hair that broke free and start the walk back up the hill to the palace. Whenever I could sneak away, I always returned to the sea.

That's how I found myself on the outcropping on the beach watching the ship glide closer. I wondered what it was doing here. This wasn't a harbor and there should be no ships coming in to dock. I squinted into the sun to get a better look and realized with horror that this was a pirate ship, not one of my father's fleet. It wasn't safe for me to be here, so close to the beach, but it was too late for me to leave unseen. Or perhaps I was too curious. I pressed myself down into the sand behind the rock and watched as the ship pulled forward to the shallow banks.

A breeze ruffled the tall grass next to me, and it was unusually quiet. A chill crawled up my arms. Something wasn't right with this ship. Then, I saw it. Instead of pulling tight with the wind, the sail was bound. Vines, clustered with grapes, circled the sail and twined around the mast. I should have been hearing the shouts of sailors clamoring to drop anchor or the slap of oars in the water, but there was nothing. Just the soft lapping of water against the ship as it bobbed in the surf.

A roar cut through the silence sending my heart into my throat. The anchor splashed - unnecessarily perhaps because the bottom of the ship had to be almost touching the soft sand. Heart thumping, I leaned forward and shielded my eyes from the sun, but I still didn't see any pirates. A lone helmsman watched from the deck, staring as if frozen. As the ship swayed in the shallow water, red liquid flowed over the decks and down the sides of the ship, turning the clear water a milky pink. At first, I thought it was blood, but then I caught the fruity scent in the breeze. It was wine. My breath caught. I crouched behind the rock, ready to run. A princess would bring a good ransom and whatever was happening on that ship, I was not going to get caught.

I waited for the pirates to climb down the ladder

and swarm the beach. Nothing. Instead, a golden lion leaped from the gangplank, his muscles taut and his mane wild. He pounced into the shallow water, padded onto the sand and shook the water from his fur. He amber eyes locked on to me. I should have been afraid, but I wasn't. Instead, I felt in awe of him, amazed at his power and beauty. His eyes held mine and I didn't notice as the ship disappeared. A splash in the distance startled me and I turned, my focus caught by the dolphins playing in the waves and when I turned back, the lion was gone. In its place stood a man with the same natural power, loose, shiny hair, and warm, sharp eyes. The tunic over his broad shoulders was ordinary, but his purple cloak shone like an amethyst. He could have been a mirage, but he stood like a king. Or a god.

Before I realized what I was doing, I stepped out from my hiding place.

"You are not afraid of me," he said, walking toward me, a faint smile playing on his lips.

I stared into his face, unable to look away. The water lapped on the beach behind him.

As he studied my face, I felt his eyes sweep across my body. Under the hot sun, his gaze felt cool on my skin. I was suddenly conscious of my breathing.

"You are Ariadne, daughter of King Minos."

"Yes. Dionysus."

His name popped into my thoughts and I knew it to be true. My mind raced with uneasy questions about why he was here and what happened to the pirates.

"You know me," he said, breaking into a grin.

Quickly, I remembered myself and knelt before him.

"Of course, my lord. Tales of your great deeds are everywhere, even our small island."

In truth, the few tales I had heard of him were frightening--stories of either frenzied, wine-soaked rites or vengeance. We had many temples, but none celebrating this erratic new god. He laughed, not the false laugh of gods, but a genuine laugh that crinkled his eyes. He motioned for me to rise and I once again looked into his face. He brushed a wayward hair out of my eyes and drew his cool finger along my jawline. His touch on my skin stopped my breath and shot warmth through my core.

"Soon you will hear more of me, Ariadne of Knossos. You will come to my temple." It was not a question.

I was stunned and speechless. Before I could answer or ask him what he meant, he turned and sauntered toward the woods. The air shimmered where he had stood and my cheek glowed warm where his skin touched mine.

The empty ship bobbed on the water. I bolted for the palace, wanting to scream and knowing I could tell no one.

I rounded the corner of the women's courtyard and ran straight into my old nurse, Alcina, who instantly narrowed her eyes.

"Where have you been?" she demanded.

I paused a moment to catch my breath and think of something plausible. Alcina took care of me for as long as I can remember. When I was hurt or upset, Alcina's were the arms I flew to for comfort. She knew me. So, it was impossible to lie to her. Instead of trying, I stayed silent and avoided her eyes. Still, I could feel her looking at me, pulling the truth out.

She put her hands on her hips and looked down at the wet edges of my dress. "You've been to the beach." It wasn't a question. I opened my mouth, but before I could speak, she interrupted - "No, don't lie to me. I know you've been there. Did you bring a guard?"

I slid my eyes away from her.

"Ariadne!"

"I know."

"What were you thinking? It's not safe for you out there by yourself."

"It's safe. Nobody would harm me."

She shook her head. "There was talk of a pirate ship spotted off the coast."

I started to protest, but she raised her hand to silence me.

"A pirate ship, Ariadne. You know what they would do with you. You aren't a girl anymore. You need to stop acting like a child."

"But- "

"Stop. What would you have done if someone

attacked you?"

"Um." I paused, thinking. "Nobody would attack me."

"You don't know that. If it happened, there is nothing you could have done. You would have been taken. How do you expect to fight off one person or worse, a group of people?"

I looked down and walked with her in silence. I couldn't argue with Alcina because she was right. When I was a child, pirates circled our shores. Not anymore. My father made sure of that. Even so, it was foolish of me not to run when I saw the pirate ship.

~ 2 ~

Having said her piece, Alcina left me alone with my pile of sewing, mainly things that needed to be mended since I usually left the design work to Phaedre. I had no interest in creating dresses, but I could often stay focused long enough to repair holes and sew seams. After everything that happened, I was glad to be alone with my thoughts, which kept coming back to Dionysus and how I felt when he looked at me, like he truly saw me. It made me flush to think of how I talked so boldly to him. I wondered if he thought of me, but decided that was foolish. Why would he? He was a god. A good looking god. Well, good looking in a lazy way and I wasn't like Persephone or any of the other beautiful maidens the poets sang about. I pushed him out of my mind over and over and tried to focus on the task at hand, which was shortening one of my mother's old dresses. I smoothed the airy fabric and decided to fit it for Phaedre.

Rather than cut the fabric, I folded it over and secured it in place. There was one thing that bothered me. Why didn't I run when I saw that pirate ship? I should have been afraid. After all, I knew the destruction caused by pirates on our shores. As a young girl, I sat next to my mother in her throne room and listened to our people tell stories of pirates murdering their husbands, stealing supplies, and destroying their homes. Fear turned to anger when our people started questioning the strength of their king, who either couldn't or wouldn't protect them from this danger. The memory of how my father dealt with it will always be with me.

He turned his greatest soldiers loose on the shoreline. Of course, they had no trouble finding pirates. They weren't hiding. Pirates have no respect for the gods other than the god of the sea and they aren't used to being challenged, at least not by fishermen and tradesmen. After sacking one of our villages, the pirates sloshed drunk around the town, while the bodies of our Cretan men lay where they were slain. The women and children who hadn't fled or been captured cowered in corners.

Our soldiers could have easily killed them all, but

that wasn't their mission. They were supposed to collect them, not kill them. In the end, the soldiers rounded up a handful of pirates and locked them in the dungeons before bringing them before the king, my father. Instead of receiving them in his Throne Room, where he would typically handle things of this nature, he held court in the outdoor theater, where we held public events. It was ideally situated for spectacle, with the palace to the south overlooking the mountains. I loved going to the theater. It meant there was going to be a show.

I held up the bottom of the skirt, annoyed to see my seam was crooked. With a sigh, I started ripping out the stitches to begin again.

When the news spread of the pirates' capture, hundreds of people flocked to the steps of the theater to see justice served. As the royal family, we sat in the back, where the two wings of the theater meet, but my father stood in the center. As soon as the guards brought in the pirates, the place erupted with the enraged shouts of people standing and shaking their fists, yelling for justice. The king raised his hand, silencing them.

I studied the pirates. Out of context, they didn't look menacing. They looked dirty. There were five total and one of them was a young boy, about my age. I searched his face to see the evil he must be filled with, but all I saw was fear. Our eyes met and I quickly looked away. The older pirates masked their feelings better, trying to stand tall and look defiant. I studied the boy, wondering where he came from and who his mother was. Where she was. While the others stood, staring hard at the king, the boy fidgeted, glancing at me or the ground.

"Pirates," my father shouted, addressing the crowd, "have made our shores unsafe. They have stolen from us and razed our villages. It stops today." Cheers erupted from the crowd.

"People of Crete. Minstrels sing songs of our bravery and victories in battle. But, our warriors grow bored with no wars to fight. It's time to take them to the sea to reclaim our coasts. We have the ships. We have the warriors. We are taking our coast back," he roared. The crowd stood, cheering in support of their king. With these words, my father restarted his navy. However, he was not done. Satisfied that he had the crowd on his side, his attention returned to the prisoners before him.

"Pirates," he continued, spitting out the word. "You will not terrorize my coasts anymore. The cargo you take from the ships is my cargo. When you steal from my people, you steal from me. When you take their women, you take mine. An affront to me is an affront to Crete. No more." He seemed to grow larger as all of the pirates shrunk, studying the dirt at their feet. "We must send a message." He paused, enjoying his control over the crowd. "Tonight, you will feast and tomorrow, my Minotaur will feast on you."

His words hung over the theater. I felt my mother stiffen beside me. Her back rigid, she held her head straight, never glancing at the prisoners. The crowd loved it. The air vibrated with excitement, as people yelled insults at the pirates and cheered. My father basked in it. He closed with some more words about the greatness of Crete, but I didn't hear him. I was looking at the young boy squeezing his eyes shut and fumbling to grab the hand of the pirate next to him. The man shooed his hand away like a fly.

Later that night, the palace hosted a feast in my father's dining hall. Traditionally, women did not dine with the men, except for my mother who sometimes joined my father as hostess. This time, I got to stand beside her. Alcina spent forever getting my hair just right and picking out jewelry, but I didn't care. I was so excited to be chosen to accompany my mother, especially alone without my sister, Phaedre. I knew it stung Phaedre when she was whisked away to her room with Alcina and it was all I could do not to turn my head and stick out my tongue at her as I sailed past. Thalia must have noticed because she stifled a smile as my mother ushered us out.

I was thrilled to be in my father's dining hall. I loved the high ceiling and the paintings of battles and heroes that covered the walls, telling the stories of my grandparents. Instead of stopping to enjoy them like I wanted to, I trailed behind my mother, studying her movements and trying to match them. Emulating my mother was not an easy task. She walked into every room like the only thing it was missing was her. My father loved showing off her beauty and watching her charm his guests, which she did effortlessly. She knew everybody and made each one feel as if he were her favorite person there. I did the best I could, smiling when looked at and trying not to fidget. It was enough.

As the princess, my role was to be seen. That was also the role of the pirates, who stood shackled in the front of the room, directly below the giant bronze double axes. By this time, the scent of roasted goat and fresh bread swept through the palace making my mouth water. I stood silently beside my mother, inclining my head appropriately and smiling when addressed.

I looked over at the pirates, who had obviously been to the baths. The layer of grime and dirt that protected them was gone and they just looked like men. Not men who pillage and strike fear. Only men, out of place and afraid, shackled together, rough against the smooth marble of the walls. Were they also thinking of the roasting goat? Or were their minds on the feast tomorrow? Their bluster gone, they stood like statues. Stories of our Minotaur circled for years and they knew what was in store for them. The only one who moved was the boy. He looked around, rocked from foot to foot, and tapped his fingers on his legs. When his eyes locked into mine, I gasped. In that instant, we didn't seem so different. I felt connected to him, to his fear and his panic. The sweet smell of the roasting meat turned sour as my stomach dropped. I looked away, breaking our connection, but before I knew it, I was speaking.

"My King, what of the boy?"

My mother's head snapped toward me, her brows narrowing in disapproval. "Ariadne," she snapped, the word echoing.

My father stopped his conversation and everyone looked at me. The room fell silent.

"Well, he's pretty small," he said. "Definitely not a whole meal. Perhaps my Minotaur will have him for dessert." Laughter erupted in the hall, but my father's laugh didn't reach his eyes. His face was hard, his jaw tight. It was too late to turn back, so I took a deep breath and continued down my path, willing my voice not to waver.

"Might we show him mercy? Send him back to the pirates to tell the tale of your strength and power? Put fear in them," I asked. My mother snatched my hand, crushing it in her grasp.

Heat crept up the back of my neck and the walls felt close, but I stood my ground. My father turned to me and thundered. "Mercy! You beg for mercy? I am the greatest king Crete has ever seen. What do you know about striking fear, you foolish girl? You forget yourself." Realizing what I had done, I clamped my mouth shut. What was I thinking questioning him in front of his guests?

He turned to my mother. "Pasiphae! Get her out of my sight!" He raised his hand, dismissing us and turned back to his guests.

My mother sprang forward. Still holding my hand, she curtsied to the king and pulled me out of the room, her pale eyes blazing.

My mother didn't say anything all the way back to our quarters. She stared straight ahead and plowed forward. When we got to my room, Alcina and Thalia jumped to attention. Their sewing fell to the floor. My normally poised mother was rigid as steel and furious. When she ordered Thalia to go check on the dinner, Thalia scurried away, shooting me a relieved, but sympathetic look. My heart pounded in my ears.

When she turned on me, the words tumbled over each other, "My Lady, I don't know why I said that. The boy. He's so young. I just felt bad for him. Surely–"

The crack of her hand against my face felt like fire. Stunned, I recoiled. Her hand print was hot on my cheek and the smack echoed in my ears.

"Ariadne. That boy is a pirate. A criminal. It is not your place to argue with your father." She looked hard at me. "And in front of guests. What could you have been thinking? You humiliated yourself. You humiliated me. He is the King! For a pirate urchin."

"I'm sorry, mother," I responded, my eyes pleading. "It won't happen again." I spun around, dismayed to see Phaedre standing in the doorway, witnessing my shame.

"It won't," she said, picking up the switch from the corner of the room and handing it to Alcina, who took it with a tentative hand.

"Ten." She turned on her heel and left the room, her silver wrap floating behind her like mist.

Without a glance back, Phaedre followed close on her heels, trying to make the sway of her hips match my mother's.

Alcina's arms folded around me as I crumbled into her. She held me as I sobbed, tears rolling down my face. I told her about the boy and what I did, what I said. When I calmed myself, she wiped my tears away and kissed my forehead. She said she was proud of my kind heart, but she needed to issue my punishment. I knew that if she didn't, my mother would visit it upon her. My heart banged in my chest as I let my tunic fall. The air was cold on my bare skin. Each lash of the switch bit like a snake and with each one, more tears flowed. It was searing pain mixed with hot shame. When she had given the requisite ten, she gently washed my back, bound the wounds, helped me into my sleeping clothes and held me again as I sobbed. When my mother came back to check, she was satisfied by the marks and retired in silence back to her quarters.

The next morning, the Minotaur feasted. Soldiers brought out baskets of bloody clothes and the leftover wreckage was burned as a sacrifice to Poseidon. Our shores were different after that. Although my father still patrolled, the pirates stayed away. Until today.

I shook out the dress I was working on and held it up. The bottom was now straight and my stitches smooth and even. You couldn't even really tell it was altered. I looked around, but the courtyard was empty. I'd have to show Phaedre later. I folded the dress and set it on the floor next to me and picked out the next garment, a shawl I'd torn on a tree branch. Overhead, the sun was high, but shadows broken by the pergola overhead gave the courtyard a soft warmth. It would be a beautiful afternoon to spend outside. Again, my thoughts returned to Dionysus and how he looked standing in the surf with the wind whipping his hair. I wondered about the temple he spoke of and whether I would see him again. Then, I pushed those thoughts away.

For the rest of the afternoon, I sewed while two guards perched on either side of the courtyard. They didn't seem any happier about it than I did.

* * *

The next morning, fog draped over the high walls of the central courtyard, not yet burned off by the sun. This was always my favorite time of the day, that peaceful hour when the birds start to wake while the rest of the palace sleeps. After spending the afternoon

32

and evening shadowed by the guards, I relished the opportunity to shake them. As Thalia, my maid, and I went off to the labyrinth, the guards hung back, as I knew they would, saying they'd wait at the palace. We walked silently. Thalia clutched the basket, which was filled with bread, cheese and leftovers from dinner. No meat today.

When we reached the entrance of the labyrinth, Thalia froze and held out the basket. She would go no further.

I took it from her gently and asked, "Are you sure you don't want to come with me?"

She shook her head. "Not today, lady." It was the same conversation we had every day since this task was assigned to me when I was nine years old. I kept asking because I hoped that one day she would join me, but I understood that she was afraid. Everyone was. He was scary.

The labyrinth was intimidating, self–contained and silent. The great inventor, Daedalus, built it as a circular prison to hold the Minotaur, who my mother named Asterion, and keep him away from my father. As only Daedalus could, he made it beautiful, winding and mysterious. If you didn't know what was in the middle, the entrance would beckon adventure. When my mother assigned me the task of feeding Asterion, I spent hours with Daedalus learning how to navigate the labyrinth. Now, with Daedalus gone, I was the only one who knew how to get in and come back out alive. Although, I had sometimes seen my mother sneak quietly inside when she thought nobody noticed. Day after day, I walked the silent paths of the labyrinth alone.

Today, the honeysuckle climbing the walls added a sweetness to the thick, heavy air. I reached out to touch a petal of the soft white flowers and then picked a couple, adding them to the basket. Unlike other areas rich with shrubs and flowers, no birds nest in the labyrinth. Like the sound between breaths, it's quiet. I padded down the circular paths, doubling back on myself and finding the rhythm of the labyrinth. It's easy to get lost in here and disoriented. That's what it was designed to do. You can't panic. He can smell fear. You need to be calm make no sudden movements. Each step is deliberate.

The maze snakes underground, leading to a natural spring under the earth. In the tunnels, it's dark and the damp walls block out all sounds. It's disorienting. Getting stuck means certain death because once you lose sight of where you are, he's smelled your fear and followed its trail. Each time, I followed the path through the underground passageways as Daedalus showed me, never deviating or exploring the nooks and alcoves.

I slowly made my way to the center, which was marked with an altar to Poseidon, the Earth Shaker. It was scratched and chipped, but still white. On either side of it, patches of wild celery grew, another nod to

Poseidon. In summer, the wide, ribbon-like leaves would be peppered with little white flowers, but not yet. As I got closer, I listened. Nothing. I walked a little forward and stopped. This time, I heard shuffling.

"Asterion," I called softly. "Brother." I never called him by any other name because I felt it spoke to the protective instincts buried deep inside him. He never responded, but I felt he knew I didn't mean him harm. After all, I brought the food. Perhaps the food is why he never harmed me, but I hoped it was because he knew we were linked, each tied to this circular prison. I waited, my breath calm, steady and shallow, my chest tight.

He shuffled in response and chuffed through his nose.

"Brother, I brought you something to eat. Do you want to come out and eat with me?" I offered, making my way to the grassy center.

Another snort. I was now in the middle and I could see him lurking behind the altar in the archway leading to the underground tunnels, where he likely lived. I wondered sometimes where he slept. Even though I wasn't supposed to, I sometimes brought blankets and other trinkets with the food. I bowed to the altar and unpacked the basket.

"There are some figs in here," I said, "I know you like those."

From the shadows, his yellow eyes followed me. I

swallowed hard and continued.

"I was down to the water yesterday. I saw the most magnificent thing." Then, remembering I couldn't tell anybody, I stopped. It was silly. Who would he tell? Still, I was afraid to say out loud what I saw. What I felt.

"Anyway, the water was bright blue and the sunlight danced off it. It goes on forever. I wonder what's on the other side. A palace like ours?" I chuckled. "Is there a girl over there wondering about us?"

He exhaled loudly and banged his hoof on the ground, making me jump. Taking the cue, I picked up the basket and backed up to the trail, never moving my eyes from the shadow behind the altar.

"All right. I hope you enjoy the figs. I'll be back tomorrow."

I walked backward until I could no longer see his yellow eyes. Then, I turned and scurried back the way I came.

After all the years feeding him, he still made my heart pound. He was unpredictable. I rounded my way to the entrance, where I found Thalia waiting for me. She looked me over and seemed satisfied. We clasped hands and made our way back to the Queen's quarters.

When we arrived at the palace, my mother was already in the receiving room. Every week, she opened her doors to the local women to hear complaints, mediate disputes and offer advice. As her daughters, Phaedre and I sat at her side. Unlike my father's throne room, which was rigid and formal, hers was open and inviting. Benches with pillows lined the walls and there were always large vases of flowers. Today, the sweet, spicy smell of wild orchids filled the room. It glowed with morning sunshine. Golden light bounced off the walls, which were covered in vivid frescoes of dolphins and dancing women. There were no pictures of bulls in this room.

My mother sat tall on her stone throne, knowing she was the most powerful woman in the room. The material in her pale blue skirt matched her eyes, which studied each woman. One by one, they came forward and knelt before her.

Thalia and I slipped in and stayed off to the side. Phaedre usually sat regally at our mother's side, but today she was absent, which surprised me. She never missed an opportunity to be seen and petted. I wondered where she was, but a part of me savored beating her here and hoped my mother noticed. It didn't happen often. Our role here was to be seen. And learn. We'd listen to the women and watch as our mother dispensed advice and sometimes herbs, talking to each one. Sometimes, they just needed to be heard. Everyone does. We had education in entertaining and running a household, but this was where we learned to be queens.

During the year of the sweating sickness, we

dispensed so much honeysuckle that our garden was almost depleted. Mothers, bold with fear for their sick children, lined up for help and my heart broke, knowing we couldn't save them all. Once, a woman came in still cradling her dead baby and begging for a cure. My mother gently told her it was too late and there were no herbs to do what she sought. The woman raged with grief, clutching at my mother's robes, cursing the gods, begging her to help. Her pain ripped through me and I felt so helpless in the face of such sadness. My mother never shed a tear. Neither did Phaedre. When I started to cry, my mother was furious. She pulled me from the receiving area, scolding that crying was common and princesses cannot show such weakness. Our people have to see strength from their palace. I was not allowed back in until after the sickness had passed through. I was glad.

Now, the woman kneeling before my mother was heavy with pregnancy and spoke in quiet words that I couldn't hear. As she wiped her nose and stifled a sob, my eye caught my mother's. She motioned for me to come forward with a flick of her hand and whispered to a servant, who went to check the herb chest. The servant returned empty-handed and after some more whispering, my mother signaled to an attendant to help the woman stand and promised to send someone around with a tincture. A servant ushered the pregnant woman out and gave her some bread, as was the custom.

I took my place next to my mother and watched as woman after woman approached. Some had babies or small children in tow and we listened to everyone. She gave thoughtful advice, or packets of herbs or tea or a poultice for their pains. The last woman approached and knelt before my mother. Her tunic was coarse wool, but she was clean. Unlike the others, she looked directly at my mother, not at her feet, but at her face.

"Lady, my Queen," she began. My mother nodded and gestured for her to continue. The woman looked down at her hands, which I saw were shaking. "My husband is a good man. He works hard making jewelry that makes everyone it touches more beautiful. The things he creates would make Hephaestus proud." She stopped.

"So, why is it you have come to see me?" my mother prompted, gesturing for her to continue.

"His eye wanders. I am … getting older and our children are growing." She placed a hand on her belly. "There will be no more. There are young girls–whores, who circle around him." She stopped again, narrowing her eyes. "They will take everything from me."

My mother took her hand and said gently, "Do not worry. I will help you."

She beckoned to a servant and whispered instructions. The servant scurried to the chest and came back with a clay jar. The servant handed the jar to my mother, who cupped it in her hands, closed her eyes and whispered a chant to Hera, goddess of all wives. She opened her eyes and handed the jar to the woman, who watched this process with wide eyes.

"Pray to the goddess Hera for aid and provide offerings at her temple. She will know your cause. Then, put some of this in your husband's tea with a little honey." This was a remedy my mother dispensed often. It was whispered that she used magic on my father to keep him faithful and I sometimes wondered if she snuck some into his tea as well, but I knew that was ridiculous. He wouldn't need herbs to stay faithful. There was no woman more beautiful than my mother.

The woman took the jar and tucked it into the folds of her shawl. "Thank you, my Lady Queen," she said. My mother signaled for her to rise and a servant escorted her out and gave her bread like the others.

After she had gone, my mother turned to me.

"Ariadne," she said.

I lowered my eyes and head. "Lady."

"Ariadne, my stocks run low. We need some dittany to aid in childbirth and ironwort for the calming tea. Please go to the mountain to gather the herbs." Although this could easily be done by a servant, my mother knew my restless spirit and sometimes indulged my longing for open spaces.

"Yes, mother," I said, trying to keep my face still. "I

shall be happy to go. I will bring Thalia and we will not return without what is needed." She nodded and I was dismissed.

Thalia and I ran back to my quarters to change into simple tunics and gather our things.

The fog burned off, revealing blue skies and the long path before us, alive with possibilities. Inside the walls of the palace, every moment was scripted. Outside was wild. We breathed and ran and giggled. Baskets in hand, we followed the road, kicking a rock back and forth as we went.

"Thalia," I asked. "What of Darius?"

She slid her eyes over to me without turning her head. "What of him?" She kicked the rock to me.

"I recently saw him digging in the garden. He's not the same skinny boy we played chariots with as children, though his curls are the same." I smiled slyly and kicked the rock back. She pretended she didn't know what I was talking about. So, I kept on. "I've heard he has a fondness for orchids." Still nothing. "Like the beautiful orchid you brought in to our room."

Thalia's cheeks grew pink and a smile spread across her mouth, lighting up her beautiful almond-shaped eyes. She signed heavily. "Fine. How long have you known?"

I laughed. "I didn't. I just thought maybe. You must tell me everything. He has gotten so handsome. That short tunic." I made a fanning motion with my hand

and pretended to swoon.

She swatted my arm and giggled. "He is handsome. And kind. He comes with me to the market sometimes if his duties allow. Mama doesn't like for me to go alone. It's not safe. At first, I couldn't even look at him. Now, we are easy, like when we were younger."

As a boy, Darius was assigned to the stables, tending the horses. Although I couldn't ride, I loved to watch my brother and the other boys in their lessons. Thalia and I spent many hours in the fields around the stables following Darius around. Whenever a horse got wild, Darius could calm him. He'd place a firm hand on the horse's neck and speak gentle, soothing words and soon, as if they understood, the horse would soften under the security of his hand. What he had with horses was magic.

Sometimes, after my brother finished training and the horses were back in their stables, we stayed around, making up games and talking to Darius, who was a little older than us and seemed so wise. He would tell us stories about chariot races and Amazons and we would pretend to be Amazons riding horses, running wild with our hair whipping in the wind. Darius even made us swords out of sticks, which we hid from my brother so he wouldn't take them away. When I think of my childhood, I summon the spring air fresh on my cheek as I ran wielding swords with

Thalia. Free. As I got older, I had things to do that were more "suitable" and didn't involve the thunder of hooves on the ground or dusty air of the stables. Darius faded into the background. Seeing her face at the mention of Darius, I was glad for Thalia, glad she had him back.

"Is he much changed?" I asked, kicking the rock back. It rolled past Thalia, disappearing into the brush.

"Not much. His voice is lower, but he's still gentle and kind. And still afraid of heights," she laughed, brightening her face. She took my hand and added,"and I bet he's still good with his hands."

Giggling, we took off running toward the forest. Out of breath and still laughing, we entered the canopy of trees, slowing our feet and inhaling the fresh, pine-scented air. I loved the quiet of the forest and that we were alone. Here, we could be loud if we wanted and nobody would mind. We could wade in rivers and throw stones and not have to keep our eyes down and our voices soft. We could just be. But, content with the subtle beat of our footsteps, we walked in comfortable silence. The leaves rustled overhead and sunlight sprinkled patterns on the trail. Overhead, a bird announced our arrival.

We walked like this until our baskets were heavy with thyme, lavender and sage. We still had not found the dittany. For that, we needed to head higher toward the rockier areas of the mountain.

I was glad Thalia remembered my shawl. Clouds were blowing in overhead and the mountain air would have a bite. I never thought of such things ahead of time, but Thalia always did. As we climbed higher, the path grew rockier, making it difficult to balance. Our breath turned ragged and my legs started to burn.

After about an hour of searching around craggy trees and over boulders, we finally found the soft little bushes, clustered in and around some large rocks ahead. Thalia put her basket down and scrambled up the boulders. I stayed a bit behind. When she was secure, I handed her my basket and she filled it, taking care with the stems and the delicate velvety leaves. She came down with a sprig behind her ear. "Perhaps, I will take this and make a tea for Darius," she said playfully, for dittany was known to be a favorite of Aphrodite.

"Oh, you don't need it," I said smiling, taking the stem from her ear and putting it back in the basket. "You are the only love potion he needs."

I looked up, noticing the sun was on its way down. We had been so intent on our task, we didn't notice the light fading and the blue sky changing to gray. "It's getting late. We should turn back."

While we were out, afternoon melted into evening. We'd wandered further from home than we planned. The trees grew still without a breeze to play with and the air was muddy and thick. Overhead, through the tree branches, clouds swirled and darkened. The shadows disappeared.

Slowly, we made our way back through the rocky hillside, careful not to spill our baskets. Thalia started to shiver when the first drop fell, but insisted she was fine. Without the warm sun, the air was cooling rapidly. Thalia remembered my shawl, but didn't bring one of her own, so we huddled inside it together, making our way back down.

One drop turned into many and soon we were soaked. Wet and shivering, we sloshed through the mud, careful around the slippery rocks.

"I think we need to wait for the rain to stop." Thalia said. "The hill gets steep and these rocks are slippery." She pointed in the direction of a cavern, opening between the rocks. "We can wait there." Confined spaces made me uneasy, but I agreed that we needed to stop for a bit.

Huddled together under my shawl, we made our way over to the cave, which was bigger than we thought. The mouth was huge, resembling an uneven arch, with enough of an overhang to keep us dry. Tentative, we called into the opening, hoping for an echo, but the darkness swallowed our voices. Inside, it was enormous. We could easily walk inside without crouching, but I had no desire to find out how deep it went or to walk blindly through the darkness. Without a torch, it was pitch black in the cave. We had no other choice, and went in just deep enough to block the wind and get out of the rain.

We settled in and sat shivering under my shawl. Rain dripped from the entrance, but at least we were covered.

"Perhaps we can build a fire?" Thalia suggested.

I was ill-equipped to build a fire, but Thalia got to work, piling up dried grass and leaves she found under a pine tree. She was always self-sufficient, doing what needed to be done. Admiring her adept movements, I felt both grateful for her and a little ashamed. As much as I loved being outside, surviving overnight in a cave was beyond anything I'd learned. Still, I could help look for sticks. So, we both ventured out to search for dry kindling. Crawling under trees and brush, we found a modest pile of needles and twigs that weren't too wet. Since we didn't want to smoke ourselves out of the cave, we started a pile right at the entrance, under the overhang just outside the cave. We stacked our kindling up around the dried grass and leaves and Thalia crouched in front of it, concentrating. She held one stick upright between her palms and rested it against a bigger stick nestled in our small pile of leaves. With a sigh, she rubbed her hands together, spinning the stick into the bigger one.

We both stared at the sticks swishing together, willing smoke to appear, but nothing happened. Over and over, she tried. Still no smoke. No fire. When her hands hurt too much to continue, she had to take a break and I tried. I was unsuccessful as well and we sat in silence, staring at the pile of twigs where our fire should be.

Now, it was dark, the moon hiding. Rain pelted down, leaving puddles in the dirt at the entrance of the cave. We scooted further inward. Inside, it was dry, but cold. We had my shawl, but without a fire, it would be a long night.

My stomach growled, a reminder that we hadn't eaten in several hours. Thalia reached into her basket and pulled out some bread and a hunk of cheese. We ate in silence, huddled together. My toes were numb, lifeless lumps. Next to me, Thalia's black hair hung in wet clumps, unable to dry in the damp air.

"We'll be all right," I said, trying to reassure us both. "It's just one night. In the morning, it will be better." She nodded, not looking at me.

A crack of lightning ripped through the sky. Hearts thumping, we held the shawl tighter and slumped together in the darkness, listening to the wind tearing through the hillside and the patter of rain outside the cave. I wondered if anyone was looking for us. If not, it was going to be a long night. We pulled my cloak tighter and shivered together in the darkness.

With a whoosh, a breeze swept through the cave and our pile of sticks sprang to life in a riot of yellow, orange, red and blue. Crackling flames licked the wood, bouncing light and heat off the walls. After a moment of stunned silence, I dropped the shawl and ran outside, frantically searching for him in the darkness. Outside the cave, grapevines, strong and green, spread over the rocks. Rain pelted me, but I barely felt it. I knew he was there. I could feel him. I looked all around the cave, but there was nothing, only rain and darkness. My heart pounded. Where was he?

"Dionysus," I whispered into the storm. His name tasted like wine on my lips.

When I came back inside, soaked and dripping, Thalia stared at me, mouth open. The story of the beach and the lion and the ship poured out of me. I couldn't hold it in anymore. I told her everything. How it felt. How I ran away. When I finished, she looked at me smiling, the light bouncing off her beautiful face. "Well, it seems I'm not the only one with an admirer."

Somehow, after telling it to Thalia, it became real. We talked and giggled and then eased into a sleepy calm. Soon, the fire smoldered into glowing embers. Feeling safe and warm, huddled together, we talked all night, drifting in and out of sleep on the hard ground.

In the morning, the sun's fingers reached into the cave to wake me. The rain moved on, leaving everything clean and fresh. Even though the fire had long burned out, the cave still felt warm. I went outside and inhaled the clean scent of sunshine on wet leaves. I touched the broad leaves of the grapevines, where overnight, fragrant bunches of grapes grew heavy, causing the vines to slump over on the rocks. I picked one of the grapes and popped it in my mouth, enjoying the burst of sweetness. I didn't want to wake Thalia, so I sat on a rock outside, enjoying my grapes and watched the morning forest wake up. The birds called to each other, their morning song happy and light. The sky blushed orange to the east and warm sunlight filtered through the leaves. It felt like a new world.

I heard rustling and the soft tread of footsteps and jumped to my feet. Was it him? I peeked into the cave. Thalia was still asleep, wrapped in the shawl. I smoothed my wild hair and looked around. At first there was nothing, but then I heard the gravel crunch. I looked around, scanning the shadows of the trees, but didn't see anything. Suddenly nervous, I ducked back in the mouth of the cave.

To my surprise, what peeked around the opening wasn't Dionysus. It was a young girl smoothing the grapevines with her hands. She stepped back when she saw me, her hand at her chest. I put my hand up and tried to tell her it was all right, not to be afraid. She was dressed oddly in animal skins with an ivy wreath on her wild, loose hair, but she studied me like I was the one out of place. "He was here," she said, her yellow eyes fixed on me.

I answered simply. "Yes."

"I must tell the priestess. This is where we will build it."

"Build what?" I asked.

"His temple, of course," she replied like it was the most obvious thing.

"What family are you from?" I asked. Often, well-born girls were sent to the temples to train to be priestesses, but this girl looked like she grew up in the forest, not the house of a nobleman. I wondered who took care of her and how she came to be wearing rags in the woods.

"No family. Just my mom. He is our family. Yours too. Come to the temple." I started at her echo of what Dionysus said when we met at the beach.

"When?"

"You'll know." She scampered off into the woods as quiet as a deer.

I stayed outside until Thalia woke. I didn't tell her of the strange girl. I don't know why. It was our first secret.

~ 3 ~

It was still early when we arrived back at the palace and I found Alcina pacing the halls. When she saw us, I didn't know if she was going to hug us or murder us. The look on her face could have gone either way. In the end, she squeezed Thalia until she didn't look angry anymore. I melted into her arms as well, happy to see her and enjoying the safety there. After properly scolding us for being out all night long, she kissed us on our cheeks and sent us off to do our chores.

In the kitchen, the basket of food for Asterion was waiting for me. I grabbed it, along with some lavender we picked in the forest and headed for the labyrinth. I would clean up when I got back. Since

Thalia had other duties to attend to, I went alone, which was perfect. I was grateful for the chance to work through my thoughts and make sense out of what happened in the forest.

Inside the labyrinth, I let my feet guide me through the familiar turns, their steady beat quieting my mind. My thoughts kept coming back to this strange new god with the amber eyes and reckless hair. Why was I drawn to him when I should have feared him? Gods are brutal and vengeful. They take what they want. To the gods, people are sport, playthings to be manipulated and moved around as it suits them. When mortals mix with the gods, it rarely turns out well for us. Still, he was only half god. His mother was a mortal, used and discarded by Zeus. No. I should stay away from him, half mortal or not, he was dangerous. But, then why did I feel safe with him? I shook my head. Next to him was probably the least safe place I could be. My mother was right about this. But yet...

I walked the labyrinth, absorbed in my conflicted heart and not paying much attention to ground. At first I didn't notice as tiny blue flowers sprung up through the dry dirt floor, lighting up the path before me. When I stopped, I saw them all around, crawling up the wooden walls and mixing with the ivy already growing there. In the shadows, they glowed bright like stars. I spun around looking for him, my heart thumping, but I was still alone.

He was different. Something inside of me called out to him and he heard it and answered with beauty. Not violence. Not possession. Beauty. I didn't understand this god, but I couldn't stop thinking of him. I was glad my feet moved on their own through the labyrinth because I wasn't paying attention and I couldn't stop smiling.

When I neared the center, I snapped back into focus. I didn't see Asterion. I heard him. First, a snort. Then, the scraping of his hooves in the dirt as he paced back and forth, restless. I called softly to him and crept closer. "Brother, I'm here."

He stopped moving, snorted once and exhaled, his hot breath mixing with the cool morning air. I could feel his yellow eyes follow me. I turned the last corner and found him waiting in the center.

The sight of him always startled me. The size of him alone was breathtaking. Although I wasn't necessarily afraid of him, I was cautious. His body was that of a man, strong and lean, with fur starting at his head and thinning down his body, ending in the rope tail of a bull. He wore a loincloth and nothing else, though I'm not sure why. He didn't care about modesty. Everything about him was savage. His head was that of a bull, with hollow eyes and sharp horns. The thick hair on the back of his neck reminded me of a mane, but instead of being shiny and thick, it was matted and dirty. Unlike a bull, he stood upright, making him seem even more hulking. Even not moving, he filled the space. His yellow eyes fixed on me as I crept closer. He watched me silently.

I broke the heavy silence between us as I fidgeted with the basket. "Thalia and I went to the mountains to gather herbs for our lady mother. Storms came and we spent the night in a cave. I brought this back for you." I held out the lavender and set it near the altar in the center of the labyrinth. "I know you like lavender and it will help you sleep." His eyes followed every step I took. His tail twitched, making me jump.

I emptied the basket of food near the lavender, but I didn't move. Neither did he. I started prattling on about our walk in the woods, describing the sights and sounds and smells of the wet dirt, pine needles, and herbs and the feel of the wind on my face. I kept talking, filling the void, as he stood still, listening. After I described the cold, damp cave and the fire that warmed it, I backed up the way I came. Understanding my story was finished, he lumbered to the altar, took the lavender and some food in his hands and retreated into the labyrinth's corridor that made his home. When he was out of sight, I exhaled all my stored breath and told him I would see him tomorrow. I backed further up the path, watching where he was and careful not to make sudden movements.

On my way out of the labyrinth, I picked the blue flowers and put them in my basket. They would be

54

perfect plaited into a wreath for my hair or placed in a vase in my room, near Thalia's orchid.

* * *

The next few months wove together without incident. I looked for signs of him everywhere, but there were no spontaneous flowers bursting from unexpected places. In fact, with the heat of summer, most of the flowers disappeared. Only the tough remained. Life had resumed where it left off. After a while, I stopped looking.

Traders came home from their journeys with many tales of distant lands and adventure. Thalia brought their stories back from the market and I wanted to hear them all. One day, as we sat weaving, she told me one that seemed familiar about a new god, captured by pirates, who freed himself, turned into a lion and killed the pirates.

As it went, the pirates kidnapped him, mistaking him for a wandering prince in his purple robes, an easy target that would command a high ransom. He let himself be captured because he thought it would be amusing. Only a god would find it amusing to be captured and tied to the mast of a ship.

One of the sailors saw something divine in him and tried to persuade the others to let him go, but they didn't listen. Instead, the pirates tied him tighter with more ropes. Now annoyed, the god freed himself.

Still, the pirates didn't recognize the god right in front of them. They tried again to subdue him, but now the god was no longer amused.

At this point in the story, Thalia paused to make sure I was paying attention. Vines erupted from the sea and entangled the ship. He turned into a lion and lunged at the pirates. I gasped. I remembered the beautiful, wild lion from the beach and found I had no trouble imagining Dionysus in that form flinging pirates overboard.

I cringed when Thalia said he ripped some of them apart. Why would he not just escape and leave them be? Only the sailor who tried to intervene on his behalf remained. After the lion leaped onto the beach and turned my world upside down, that remaining sailor made it safely to the next port.

"What?" I asked, stopping my weaving in mid-row when I felt Thalia looking at me.

"Did you hear me? He killed them all."

"Not all. He left the one who saw him for what he was."

"Ari," Thalia said, shaking her head. "He tore them apart."

My mouth went dry. I knew she was right. I should be appalled, frightened even.

"Well, they did kidnap him…" I offered, though I knew it was a weak excuse.

"Just be careful," she said, laying her hand over mine. "I don't want you to get hurt."

Or torn apart, I thought.

Instead of responding to her concern, I changed the subject, asking if there were more stories of him, hoping for something a little less bloody. She shrugged and said that aside from a few stories about a stranger helping farmers with their crops, there weren't any.

Satisfied that she made her point, Thalia didn't pursue it and we continued to weave in silence, each absorbed in our thoughts.

As I sat at my loom, I tried to take my mind off Dionysus by telling myself stories about the Amazons. It was a pastime I developed when I was a child fascinated by the legendary warriors. As I sewed or wove, my imagination went wild with Amazons fighting battles. I imagined them teaching me how to shoot arrows from the back of a horse without falling off. I would sit tall, riding like my brother, proud and strong and have armor commissioned to ride into battle like Athena with Thalia at my side. In my stories, we would always return victorious.

Instead of riding horses into battle, I spent hours with my sister and mother at the loom until my back ached and I couldn't see straight. We finished the tapestry for my father and started on the shroud for the festival. It needed to be perfect for the gods, made of only the finest cloth. Thalia's hands were raw from working the wool to get it light and smooth enough for the feather weave. My mother made her poultices

57

by grinding heart-shaped tilio leaves and mixing them with aloe juice to soothe her angry skin. They helped a little and Thalia didn't complain, but I could tell her hands were still tender.

Although I didn't mind the weaving, and sometimes enjoyed sitting quietly in sync with my mother and sister or chatting with them about nothing, I was beginning to get restless. The weaving room grew close and tight. I longed to feel the wind scream through my hair and the sun on my face. Guards were posted outside the door, which my mother said was for our safety, but I suspected they were there to make sure I stayed put. Everywhere I went, guards followed. I yearned to sneak away with Thalia and breathe in the spicy air at the market and drink in the chaos of buyers and sellers.

While Thalia and Darius flirted at the market, I went to the weaving room to work on the shroud, which was starting to take shape. The cloth was so light and delicate that it reminded me of a cloud stretched thin. In contrast to the delicacy of the fabric, the picture depicted Poseidon riding a bull through the sea, holding his trident aloft as if riding into battle. I added some dolphins to give some color to the sea, as well as to honor the god who surprised me with flowers and fire. My sister, Phaedre, wound some golden thread into the water, which made it seem to sparkle in the sunlight. It would honor the gods who cared for us, but it did make me a little sad to think of finishing this beautiful shroud and then lighting it on fire, for our hard work and love to evaporate into smoke. I knew it was important. The shroud wasn't about us. It needed to honor both the gods and the people it carried to the underworld. Still, it was a lot of work and there was much to do.

After a long day of being confined, I stretched out on my mat, staring at the ceiling. My hands were sore and my vision blurry. Hours of staring intently at the cloth left me feeling like I was walking in a dream, unable to focus on anything. So, I skipped dinner and rested, my mind still in the rhythm of weaving. Thalia came in with a basket.

"Hungry?" she asked, holding out some barley bread and olives.

My mouth watered, suddenly starving. I sat up and invited her to sit down next to me. Thalia launched into a story about Darius helping one of the mares give birth. Her face radiated love and turned bright red when I commented on it. The door flew open, startling us.

"Ariadne, do you want to play dice. The ambassador's daughters – Oh." Phaedre stood at the door. At the site of Thalia, her face hardened. Thalia jumped up.

I looked between them, Phaedre's face sharp and angular, beautiful, but cold. Thalia was the opposite, soft with her olive skin and large, dark eyes. Phaedre straightened her back.

"Isn't there something you should be doing?" she asked Thalia. "I'm sure there's water to be brought up."

Thalia bowed her head and darted out of the room, eager to be away from Phaedre, who always made her nervous since that time we were children and Phaedre had her whipped.

It was horrible. When we were children, Thalia and I made up stories, using sticks for arrows and rode around on imaginary horses. Sometimes, my brother, Androgeos, would pick me up and swing me onto the back of his horse. I'd hold on for dear life and shriek with delight as he egged the horse on faster and faster. On the back of his horse, I was an Amazon, wild and free, defending my home from invaders.

Once, Thalia and I were in the middle of a story with Thalia acting the role of Queen Diodorus and I was her number one warrior. I had no interest in playing a queen. Phaedre came upon us in the middle of the story, just as Thalia was giving me orders about a village to sack and her face went dark. Phaedre took one look at Thalia, in her crown made of branches and ran off. Later, my mother had Thalia whipped and forced me to watch. It was my fault. Each time the whip hit, I flinched and when Thalia winced, my back hurt. Alcina, with her face frozen like stone, gripped my hand as I held in the sobs, knowing the more tears I shed, the more lashes she would get. Phaedre watched too, but with a small smile on her face.

Since then, Thalia and I made sure to maintain our formal manners around Phaedre.

I rolled my eyes at Phaedre. "That wasn't necessary. She's done all of the chores assigned to her today. Besides, she's my maid, not yours."

"It's not proper for you to treat her like you do. After all, I'm your sister."

"How could I forget."

I wished it was different with Phaedre, but we didn't connect. I remember when she was born. I was elated to have a sister. Boys were wild, feral. They learned how to ride horses and hunt and how to fight. My older brother, Androgeos, went places I couldn't follow. A sister would be mine. However, even when she was a baby, it was apparent that Phaedre and I were very different. She was always fussing, loving to be petted and held and adored. Like my brother, I was happiest when I was dirty and sweaty. As Phaedre got older, she molded herself into a miniature version of our mother, mirroring her movements, sitting straight and shaking her finger at me when she thought I was misbehaving, which was often.

As we grew, we grew more apart. Phaedre listened with rapt attention to my mother's lessons on how to behave and walk and carry yourself. She was graceful. I fidgeted my way through them. I asked too many questions and not about the right things. I wasn't interested in how to properly manage a household or memory tricks to remember stranger's names. I wanted to hear stories. When ships came into port, I wanted to know where they were from and what it was like on the open sea. I wanted to know how things worked and where they came from.

Phaedre raised her eyebrow. "Whatever. Are you coming or not?"

"No. I'm tired. I just want to rest."

She huffed and rolled her eyes. Without another word, she turned around and stomped out of the room. Once she was gone, Thalia peeked around the corner. Seeing it was clear, she came back in and plopped down beside me. Thalia was unusually quiet.

"Thalia, is something bothering you?"

"No. I'm fine," she said.

"Are you sure?" I pressed.

"Yes. Just tired."

We sat in silence for a while longer and she said. "There was much talk in the market today."

"Oh? Tell me. About what?" I asked.

"Your god," she said, with a sly look.

My god. I suppressed a smile. "He's hardly mine, Thalia. Anyway, what about him."

"They say this new god has many women who follow him and a new temple has sprung up in a cave, our cave, I think. Some of these women have left husbands and children to worship him and there are unusual stories…"

"What stories?"

"Frenzied dancing and lewd acts. They say they get so wild these women have torn apart animals with their bare hands and eaten them raw." Eyes wide, her hands mimicked the action.

That was absurd. "Why would they tear apart animals? That makes no sense. It's disrespectful to the Mother." I scoffed, wondering how that could be true.

"They say they don't care. Dionysus protects them. They call the animals a sacrifice."

"A sacrifice? Without a proper altar or ceremony? Without even a fire? How could they do such things?" I said, incredulous.

She shrugged. "That is what is being said."

"What else is said?"

"That he wants to be recognized, but the gods won't because of his mortal mother. So, he's building a following and destroying those who deny him."

I looked down at the floor, suddenly not feeling hungry anymore. What did I care? He was hardly my god. He was volatile and insecure. It was good he found a tribe of followers and left me alone. I shrugged my shoulders.

Thalia glanced at me and took my hand. "There was also good," she said. "The harvest is the best it has been in years. They say it is because of him. He shows the farmers how to turn the grapes into wine. Even barren land is blooming."

"I must go market and hear for myself," I said, hungering for more information.

63

"You can't," Thalia replied. "It's not safe."

"Why is it not safe?"

"They say a warrior is coming."

"A warrior?"

"That's what they say."

"Who? Why would a warrior come here?" I asked, alarmed.

She looked at me, shrugged her shoulders. "I don't know."

A chill rolled down my back. Warriors bring war. Since my father had dominated the seas, we have lived in peace. There were scarce signs of even a single pirate, much less a warship advancing on our shores. What could a warrior want with us?

~ 4 ~

Each day, Phaedre, my mother and I gathered in the weaving room. On the surface, everything was normal. We wove and sang songs and gossiped about nothing in particular. But, something was in the air. Nobody spoke of a warrior. Yet, the guards increased outside the palace walls, while my mother quietly stocked up on healing herbs. We didn't speak of the guards or why my parents assigned task after task to keep Phaedre and I confined to the palace.

The weight of things unsaid is heavy. It's there in every conversation, every movement, making everything feel stilted and awkward. I longed for escape, to breathe in the sea and bathe my face in the salty air. After about a week of being trapped in the palace, I talked my mother into letting me accompany Thalia and Darius on a walk through the village distributing her herbs and remedies. Normally Thalia would do this on her own, but these days Darius came with her whenever she left the safety of our walls. There were six packets to deliver including a sage and lemon balm mixture for the blacksmith's son's cough, a chamomile rub for the elders' arthritis, and my mother's secret mint mixture for the mason's wife. It's said to help with her stomach problems, among other things. They didn't demand these remedies of my mother and my mother never requested payment. My mother traded in loyalty, and with each remedy, she built up her stores. Her gifts were always appreciated, and when the queen acknowledged a sick child, it was a sign of pride and favor.

Just as when I went to the market, I dressed in plain clothes and lingered back as Thalia knocked on each door to deliver the remedies. Most people didn't give me a second look, and it was lovely to observe without being watched. What's funny is that most of these people have been to the Queen's Room and knelt before her with me at her side. At the palace, they see only the ornaments. They don't see the girl. Or maybe they notice nothing aside from my mother. She does have that effect.

The blacksmith shop was our last stop because it is

farthest away, by itself at the end of the street. In the village, the houses are close-packed clusters of white stone. Some share a common courtyard, while others, like the blacksmith shop, have its own. When we knocked on one door, the neighbors all pop their heads out to see what's happening, but since the blacksmith shop was separated from its neighbors by a small field, it was quiet. Normally, kids gathered there to play, but today, the lot was empty.

The sun hammered down without even a cloud to soften it, baking the earth around us and draining my energy, leaving me wilted. A servant answered the door and showed Thalia and me to the courtyard, which was delightfully shaded. While she showed Darius to the servant area, we rested on hard benches fanning ourselves and listening to the clanging from the workshop nearby. I thought of how hot the blacksmith must be, working with fire on a day like this. After a few minutes, the blacksmith's wife bustled out and greeted us warmly. We rose to greet her.

Thalia held out the package. "This is from our Lady, the Queen, for your son. She noted when she saw you last that he was coughing terribly. This tea will help. It's made of sage, lemon balm, and echinacea root. If you serve it warm, the steam and the herbs should provide relief. The taste is not… great."

The woman smiled, clasping Thalia's hands. "I will try it. Please, thank the Queen for her kindness."

Thalia bowed her head. "I will, my lady. I pray to the gods that your son will recover quickly."

A curly haired boy of about six peeked around the corner and wandered in. His mother scooped him up, kissing his bright-red cheeks before putting him down and gesturing to us. "Galen," she said, "these ladies came from the queen with some medicine for your cough."

He peeked around her skirts and said thank you, bowing his head like a gentleman. He was so small.

Coughing seized his little body. It was a dry, ugly hacking cough, and the force of it made me wince. It was a horrible sound. I'm ashamed to say my instinct was to back away from him. Thalia's was to reach for him. When he recovered, his breath came ragged, and his eyes were wet with tears. His mother picked him up, rested her chin on his head and held him close, smoothing his hair and kissing the top of his head.

That intimate, maternal gesture touched me. I envied the easy affection bestowed upon him by his mother. For a fleeting moment, I wondered whether my mother had ever kissed the top of my head like that. Of course, she must have at some point.

He squirmed out of his mother's arms and scampered away. As he disappeared down the hallway, I bit back the fear that not even one of my mother's remedies would be enough to save him. I hoped I was wrong.

Led by the trill of the cicadas, we headed back down

the dusty road toward the palace. Even as the shadows lengthened and the sun made its descent, it was still unbearably hot. With a sideways glance at me, Darius took Thalia's hand, and she smiled up at him, her face glowing. I didn't know this dance they found themselves in. Sheltered in the palace, I was protected from the attention of the local boys. In truth, I didn't even know any. For a moment, I wondered if anyone would ever look at me the way Darius looked at Thalia, like he didn't see anything else. No, I thought with a pang, when I married, it would be someone of my father's choosing. I trailed behind them, thinking about the easy way they walked side by side and remembered the three of us as children tearing around the stables.

Now, the lines were drawn. I was the mistress and they the servants. Perhaps, they were drawn then as well, but I didn't notice. Looking at their faces, so in love, I couldn't help feel that they had something together that I would never have. I felt protective of it, but also melancholy, wondering what the future held for me. And also them.

That night, I was restless, tossing and turning as unpleasant dreams rolled over and over in my head. Images of flames on the water, ships overflowing with wine, and little Galen's big eyes fought each other. After a while, I gave up. I stared at the ceiling and waited for the first sign of light. When the sun peeked over the horizon, I got up, dressed, and went to retrieve Asterion's basket of food.

In the creamy morning light, a blanket of stillness draped around the sleeping palace. Only the servants were up and about, preparing for the day. The basket was already waiting for me, and I grabbed it and ducked out. I was tired and cranky and didn't feel like talking to anybody. Uneasy and distracted, I entered the labyrinth, but within a few turns, I found my rhythm and my mood started to lift. At the center, it was quiet, no rustling or snuffling. Asterion must have been still sleeping. I gently unpacked the basket and backed up the way I came.

As the queen, one of my mother's primary duties was running the household, and she made it seem effortless. With my mother, you didn't even realize you were being managed. Servants performed their duties as if they were part of a choreographed dance, and her feasts were famous. As we got older, she delegated some of her duties to Phaedre and me. It was far less exciting than the hunting and fighting the boys trained for.

My task today was to make sure we had enough food for the festival. So, after I fed Asterion, I headed to the storage area. This is something a servant could easily do, but my mother insisted I learn. I tried not to be sulky about it, but I'd rather be almost anywhere than in the dark, dusty storage area counting jars of food. At least it was early. Maybe, by getting an early start, I could have some free time later.

The storeroom holds all the food and supplies collected in taxes from the area farms. I hated it in there. It's dark and monotonous and when I was little, I was afraid of the shadows and what could be hiding around corners. The one thing I loved about this room was the giant jars. Some were taller than me. When I was a child, Thalia and I would play hide and seek while Alcina did the inventory. Each jar was carefully painted with its own story, etched with pieces of our history. Battles and farmers and intricate pictures.

Now, as I wove among them, I took note of what was abundant and what was lacking. Olives were plentiful, as they usually were. The corn was low, which was also typical for this time of year. Nothing unexpected or out of the ordinary. I sighed and looked around at the sea of jars.

A soft light peeked out from the next row over. Cautious, I made my way through the maze of jars to investigate. At first, I didn't see anything, but I felt it all around me. The air had a spark. My heart sped up. I knew he would be there before I turned the corner and saw him.

Dionysus stood, leaning casually against the side of a jar, grinning more like a mischievous boy than a commanding god. Even dressed in a plain tunic, he couldn't hide who he was. He didn't need the trappings of a king because that dark, intense gaze could belong to no other. I felt him in my skin, in my breath. His hair was loose, dark, and disconcertingly tussled. I had to stop myself from reaching out to smooth it down.

"Princess," he said, holding out his arms like he was addressing a crowd. I realized I was staring and bowed down before him.

He motioned for me to rise. "Please, stand, my princess." I stood.

"My lord," I greeted him, meeting his eyes, which rested uncomfortably on me.

"You are still not afraid," he said, with a hint of amusement.

"How can I be afraid of someone who brings me fire when I'm cold?"

He smiled, his dark eyes playful. "Was that me? How do you know? Perhaps it was good fortune."

"You have a certain... flair."

He laughed.

I felt my face redden. "Thank you for your help in the cave. It would have been a long night without your assistance."

He nodded.

There was an awkward beat while we stood looking at each other.

"What are you doing here? Is there something I can do to repay your kindness?" I prompted, nervous. The gods don't do anything without compensation.

"Do? No, no. I only wished to see you," he replied, looking around. "And show you something. Come with me." He held out his hand.

When he smiled, his whole face smiled. It was disarming. I looked around at the unrecorded jars. I had a job to finish. I shouldn't go with him. He was a god, for goodness sake. But, could I refuse? Did I want to? No, I definitely wanted to go wherever he went.

With a start, I realized I hadn't said anything. I'd just been standing there like a fence post, staring like an imbecile. My mouth snapped shut. He raised an eyebrow. "Well, are you coming?"

I took his hand. "Where are we going?"

He didn't answer. Breathless, I followed him out of the dark storage room and down the road away from the palace. I didn't tell anyone where I was going, and I wondered for a passing minute if I should alert someone. I brushed it away. He asked if I wanted to get a chariot, but I shook my head. I was fine right where we were. Besides, walking, we had to remain closer to the palace.

By now, the sun was high and burned through the morning haze. We crunched down the dirt road, while I snuck glances at him out of the corner of my eye. I thought I caught him doing the same. He walked with the casual confidence of someone who knew he wouldn't be challenged. When I asked again where we were going, he winked and told me it was a surprise.

The town was awake. As we got close to the village, horses clomped past us. People carrying baskets or children bustled around. For the first time, I walked through the town in my normal attire. I don't know what I thought would happen, but nobody paid much attention. If anything, I noticed that people seemed to be avoiding us. Whenever we got close, they glanced at us and went back into their houses. Sometimes, they gave a muffled greeting, but they always turned away. Nobody met our eyes. After a woman shielded her kids, I saw the fear on her face. I looked over at my companion, but Dionysus didn't seem to notice, or if he did, he didn't care. He kept walking forward, without even a sideways glance.

It made me uneasy. I thought of the stories Thalia brought back from the market. Some were good, of barren fields that suddenly flourished. However, some were dark and savage. One about King Pentheus being ripped apart by his own family after Dionysus clouded their minds, sprang to mind and a wave of cold fear washed over me. I had a burning desire to know what happened. I couldn't reconcile the god in front of me with the one who inspired such savagery.

"There is much talk of you in the village," I blurted out. "The farmers' barrels are overflowing, and they talk of the new god who helps the harvest."

"What else do they say?" he asked. The gods are always greedy for praise.

"Many things, my lord," I said, hesitating. "Strange things that I do not understand."

"Don't be shy. What don't you understand?"

I was quiet, unsure of how to ask and not sure if I wanted to know.

"No, tell me, my princess. What strangeness do you speak of?"

"There is a story of Pentheus and his um... death." I said, hoping that would be the end, wishing I hadn't gone down this path.

His dark eyes narrowed. "Ah, Pentheus, my cousin. Filled with anger and scorn, unable to see what was right in front of him. He was hateful, mocking an old, blind seer who tried to show him the truth." He paused, looking past me, and then continued. "I tried to persuade him. Show him the divine. I even allowed him to take me to his ridiculous prison. When I could see he couldn't be reached, I broke out of his chains with no bloodshed. I tried to show him wonders. Things he could never dream of. He met my efforts with mockery and insults. He could not be redeemed. His soul was dark and impure." He spoke directly like he was recounting the ending of a story, not the death of a man.

"Because he didn't bow to you?" I asked.

"Because he didn't hear when the gods spoke to him. He didn't see the divine. He only saw himself. When a ruler thinks he is greater than the gods, his people suffer." I thought of my father and how he didn't sacrifice the white bull.

"Why not just kill him then? Why have his family

rip him apart?"

"Ahh, my princess," he smiled. "Where is the story in that? Tales of his death are told everywhere. Even here. Songs are sung and lessons are learned. Pentheus got no less than he deserved, and when people sing of his death, it reminds them to honor the gods. I assure you. His people are better off."

I suspected he was right about the spectacle, but I looked down at the ground, unsure how to respond. He was a god who had the power to take people's reason and make them do things they wouldn't dream of doing on their own. I should not be here with him. It was dangerous to even walk this road.

"You are not convinced," he said. He stopped walking and turned to face me.

I met his eyes and replied. "He sounds like a terrible man, but the power of the gods is also shown through beauty, through love."

His smile brightened his face. "Indeed, Princess," he said. "Unfortunately, that's not always enough. Life is uncertain. You are right, though. It's always best to start with beauty." He held out his hand. In his palm, sprouted a bright yellow flower. He offered it to me and I took it warily and wove it into my headband. I was suddenly aware of his presence and how close we were to each other. He smelled of grape leaves and sunshine. The air stopped moving around us. He reached out and smoothed the flower, bringing his hand down over my hair and rolling his thumb across my jaw. His hand brushed my chin and his thumb grazed my lips. Warmth spread across my body. Then, he turned and continued down the path.

We continued down the road, past the close white houses of the village and into the countryside. I couldn't imagine where we were going. When I asked for the third time, he told me we were almost there. A few moments later, when we turned down a dilapidated path toward an old farm, I was surprised and a bit confused. I was expecting something grand, but this farm looked barely serviceable. A few craggy olive trees guarded the front where the soil was so dry only a splatter of spiny plants and grasses fought their way out of the cracked earth. We made our way up to the house, which sat further up the hill. There were no animal pens, which was not a surprise. Only the richest farmers housed animals. It was obvious that this farm was not a prosperous one.

As we got closer, a man came walking out of the house, arms outstretched. After the reaction of the villagers, I was a little taken aback by the openness of this farmer. He greeted Dionysus warmly, taking both his hands and welcoming him and then bowing before me. He introduced himself as Mandilari and I liked his wide-set, dancing eyes and his easy smile. He led us to the courtyard, where he offered us water and small cookies. I nibbled them out of politeness, but I felt guilty taking from him when he had so little. Looking around, it was apparent he didn't have much to offer, but to refuse hospitality would have been a grievous insult.

"Lady," Mandilari started, "I'm so honored by your visit. Thank you for coming."

I nodded. "It's my pleasure, sir. However, I have to admit. I'm a little confused about the purpose of our visit." I looked from one to the other, hoping one of them would fill me in.

Dionysus chuckled. "What do you think, Mandi? Should we show her what we've been working on?"

Mandilari popped up and gestured for us to follow him.

He led us out the back of the courtyard, which rested at the top of the hill. In contrast to the barren front of the farm, the back was a rolling hill containing row after row of fledgling vines. In the valley sat another stone enclosure. Like an excited child, Mandilari lead us to the building.

Inside, was a square basin that resembled a shallow, flat funnel. In the main room, the floor was bumpy with layers of grapes.

"This," Dionysus said, sweeping his hand across the room, "is the future of Cretan wine. We wished to show it to you and for you to be the first to crush the grapes for the first batch."

"But how did you get grapes? It's not time for the harvest yet."

He waved off my question. "Well, I have a gift for growing things. I've been teaching Mandilari how to grow the best grapes and what to do with them. So, he'll be ready when the harvest comes."

"He saved my farm," Mandilari cut in. "The last harvest was ruined. The corn barely sprouted. I didn't know what I would do. Then, he came." He beamed at Dionysus who put an arm around his shoulder and shrugged off the praise.

"Come. We did it together."

"All right," I said. "What do we do?"

A servant came from outside with a bucket of water. She tucked a gray hair into her cap, smoothed her apron and bent down to wash our feet. Her hands were rough but gentle. As she tied up the bottom of my dress, she lowered her voice and said, "Miss, this is dirty work. I'm not sure if it's fit for a princess."

It was all right, I assured her. I wasn't afraid to get a little dirty. I didn't tell her that after spending weeks in a chair spinning thread or weaving at a loom, this was a welcome change. I glanced up at Mandilari, who beamed at her with pure love. With a rush of shame, I realized that this wasn't a servant getting us ready. This was his wife. I assumed from her plain, worn clothes that she was a servant. I silently chastised myself for the oversight.

Dionysus took my hand, and the three of us stepped into the basin.

"Now, stomp," Dionysus said. "We must flatten all the grapes."

Cautiously at first, we began stepping on the grapes,

smooshing them. With each step, the grapes moved, making the ground undulate. I reached out for Dionysus to steady myself. His hand was solid and warm, and I held it for longer than I needed. As I got more comfortable, I jumped and stomped, giggling as the grapes popped and squished under my toes. Soon, the fresh smell of grapes filled the room. Juice splattered and my feet slipped over the slick floor. We laughed and held each other's arms to stay upright. Several times, I almost fell but was pulled back up laughing at the last moment. I don't think I had ever laughed so freely with anyone besides Thalia before and it felt good.

Dionysus pointed out holes in the corners of the basin where the juice flowed. I had never seen anything like this before, and I wished to see the rest. He helped me out of the basin, taking my hand so I wouldn't fall. My feet and legs were sticky, and my dress was splattered with juice, but I didn't care. We stood for a moment grinning foolishly at one another before he brought his hand up and wiped some juice off my nose. He lingered there, close to me and I was suddenly conscious of my breathing. I looked away and asked about the press.

It was an incredible design, with the juice flowing in layers to an underground pool. We walked down the steps to the room underground, which was dark and damp, but still smelled fresh like grapes. Dionysus pointed out a little canal, which carried the juice into a pool, where it collected before moving further down through a small filter that strained out the bits of skin or seeds. In the last level, the juice landed in another pool covered with smooth tiles in a mosaic resembling a beautiful tree. From there, Mandilari scooped up the juice into clay pots, where it would rest and start the fermenting process. There was an area even further underground, which would remain cool for the wine to rest. Mandilari described each step of the process, proud like a child with a new toy, while Dionysus looked on like a proud father.

I didn't know much about wine making, but I knew this was on a larger scale than anything we had on our island. The press at the palace was the size of a barrel, with room only for one pair of feet to stomp. With this press, Mandilari was correct. It would change his farm. We walked through the vines, and he named all the varieties. I couldn't wait to come back someday and taste the finished product.

Mandilari's wife helped put my unruly hair back to rights, and she was able to scrub most of the purple off my legs and feet. My dress went all the way down to the ground, so I wasn't concerned. When she finished, I looked like myself, but I felt a glow and happiness I didn't have when I arrived. I hugged her and wished her well as I left, promising to return.

On the long walk home, I wanted to know everything about what we just did. I bounced along the path, peppering Dionysus with questions. I wanted to hear stories of other places he'd traveled. I wanted to drink in the blue sky and fill myself with his adventures. I was hungry for it. I fired question after question at him, and he managed to keep up. He told me of his travels and about some of the people he met. When I asked him why he picked Mandilari instead of one of the larger farmers, Dionysus said that he picked him because he wasn't rich. He picked him because he was poor and because he recognized the beauty of the grapes and what they could do. Mandilari needed the vineyard, and the vines needed him. He would make it part of himself. As he talked, I stole glances at Dionysus and admired the way he lit up when he spoke about the wine.

We stopped at the bottom of the hill just outside the palace gates, which was the section of road not visible from the guard station. I paused and glanced back at the palace. I suddenly didn't want to go back. It was already early afternoon, and I had been gone longer than I thought. If someone were looking for me, I would be in trouble. When I paused, he asked if everything was all right. Was it? I didn't know how to tell him what was rolling through my mind, how I always felt apart from my people, but today, I didn't. He showed me part of my island that I couldn't see from the walls of the palace. With my feet in the grapes, I felt connected. To him as well. Dionysus was a puzzle I wanted to figure out. I couldn't say that. Instead, I said everything was fine.

At the gates of the palace, we stood for a moment, silence stretching between us. I didn't want to move, but I knew I had to. He stood slightly behind me, and I was glad he couldn't see my face. Without a word, his fingers grazed the back of my neck as they swept my hair to the side. In a fleeting moment, so soft I might have imagined it, he touched his lips to the base of my neck. A lightning bolt of heat ripped through my body. I spun around, but he was gone.

~ 5 ~

Jittery and excited, I ran back to my rooms, eager to find Thalia and tell her about my morning. When I got there, she informed me that my mother stopped in several times looking for me. Instead of dissecting the puzzle of Dionysus, Thalia helped me change clothes and rushed me out to find my mother. Anxiety settled into my stomach. I hoped she didn't know where I had been.

I found my mother playing dice with some of her attendants in her private courtyard. When she saw me, she brushed the attendant away and gestured for me to sit down. I sat.

When I was a child, being in here alone would have thrilled me. Today, something about the way she studied me made me uneasy. I settled into the cushion, trying to still my fidgeting hands. I was still bubbling over Dionysus, and it was difficult not to blurt out everything that had happened. After all, wasn't that the sort of thing a girl should share with her mother? One look at her narrowed brow told me that no, this was not the time. Still, excitement buzzed through me. If she looked too hard, she would see it written on my face. However, she didn't seem to notice.

My mother picked up the dice and rolled them across the tray in front of her. Frowning at the way they landed, she handed them to me. Without a word, I tossed the dice. They fell with the 4, 5, and 6 sides up, which was a good roll. I smiled at my mother as she scooped them up.

As she shook the dice in her hand, I watched the sun caress my mother's blond hair, still shiny and thick. She was the daughter of the sun god, Helios, and despite her pale complexion, she looked it. I touched my own darker, wild, curly hair escaping my headband and wondered what it felt like to have beauty handed down from a god. For several long moments, we passed the dice back and forth without speaking. I wondered why I was here, but I wasn't going to speak first. Despite my initial good luck, I was rolling poorly, but my mind wasn't on our game. My thoughts kept coming back to Dionysus and the gods. His mother was mortal and I wondered what about her had caught Zeus's eye. Maybe it was her strength, the boldness of thinking she could look upon him in his true form. Perhaps, I thought, beauty isn't everything.

Still, I wanted to know. I couldn't help myself. I tossed the dice and casually said, "Mother. There are many stories of mortals and gods coming together. You, yourself have a god for a father. How do such things happen? Surely, sometimes, there is a happy ending."

She stopped in mid-throw and looked at me like I had a horn growing out of my forehead.

"No, there is no happy ending. The gods take what they want, use what they need, and leave behind what they don't."

"But-"

"No." She cut me off, her voice rising. "What do you know of my mother? Helios took her and left her alone and pregnant. After bringing his fourth child into the world, she died bleeding and speechless and alone. No, Ariadne. There is no happy ending for girls who tangle with the gods."

I shifted uncomfortably in my seat. Her expression was iron, and I hid my eyes so she wouldn't see what was written there. I said, "Yes, mama," in a small voice like when I was a child. She nodded and tossed the dice. The matter settled, we continued to play in awkward silence. After several moments, the ice receded.

"Ariadne," she said, looking thoughtful. "You have so much of your father in you. Did you know that the first time I saw him, I couldn't speak to him?"

My mother never talked about her past. "Really?" I replied, eager for her to continue.

She tossed the dice, this time a slight smile acknowledged her roll, which won her the round. "He spoke a different language. I only knew how to say hello in his tongue." She laughed. "Not that it mattered. He wouldn't even look at me. He was just a boy, pretending to be a man to show my mother his strength. He could barely meet my eyes."

I laughed too. I couldn't picture my imposing father afraid to meet anybody's eyes.

"Before I sailed for Knossos, my mother got me a teacher to show me all the ways of Crete-the language, the gods, the history. Everything. For hours, my tutor would drill me, making sure I knew them inside and out. I hated it. I just wanted to run through the hills and olive groves of my island, and I didn't see why I had to learn such things."

She stopped and gave me a pointed look. I smiled at her, happy we had this thing in common. "When I was seventeen," she continued. "I sailed to Crete. I had never been off my island before. I might as well been moving to the end of the world. My mother kissed the top of my head, and I never saw her again. I will never forget how Colchis looked, growing smaller in the distance as my ship broke waves. I was so scared."

My mother was scared? This was news. I had so many questions, but I was afraid to speak and risk breaking the spell and ending the story.

"I was alone. Only servants came with me. Finally, we landed and stepped onto the soil. I was so glad to be off the ship. It looked so similar to my home but so unfamiliar at the same time. Only then, was I grateful for my harsh teacher because I knew the ways of this strange place as if I had been born here. At the amphitheater, I saw your father for the second time. He met my eyes then, and I greeted him in his language. He stood taller. He was so handsome. All that thick, dark hair." She smiled and smoothed my hair. I froze. "I remember his hands shaking when he took mine." She paused, smiling at the memory. "When we wed, I wore a crimson gown and we stood beneath the awning. The priests prayed to all of the gods, but I wasn't thinking of them. I was thinking of being Queen."

She stopped and took my hand. "You shall be a queen someday."

"Yes, mother," I replied, unsure of what to say.

"You need to take your place in the world, as I did so many years ago. Your father thinks it's time for you to marry. It's past due, probably. This is the year of the tribute. We will have a banquet and the interested candidates will present themselves to your father. He will choose a suitable match. I know you think I'm harsh, maybe unforgiving. Maybe I am. But it's to prepare you. Now, you're ready."

My whole life built to this moment. I'd been trained and conditioned and prepared for a husband. Still, I felt like someone punched me. I stared at her, my face expressionless, unable to form words. Finally, I muttered, "Yes, Lady." I had so many questions, but the words wouldn't come. She kept talking, but I didn't hear anything else she said.

My mind raced all the way back to my quarters, but I couldn't think. The words, "a suitable match" kept playing in my mind. Who was a suitable match?

All my life, I'd wanted to see what lay beyond our shores, but now that it was before me, all I could think was that I didn't want to leave my home. My family. My mother was right; it was time to take my place in the world. But where was that? With who? Life in the palace was about women's work-weaving, managing the servants, attending to the queen, my mother. The only men I had known were my father and brother and servants, and even that was limited. My father did not concern himself with what happened in the women's quarters. Now, I was to be paraded and gifted to a prince I had never met. What would he look like? Would I please him? What would happen if I didn't? My rib cage squeezed my chest, making it difficult to breathe.

Back in my room, Thalia rushed to meet me, her face full of concern. I fell into her and spilled the news of my upcoming marriage. Like a good friend, she put on an expression of delight and proceeded to try to fill me with optimism.

"Lady, that's wonderful news. You are going to be a queen! What beautiful princes you will bring into the world," she said, hugging me.

"I wonder who will present themselves..." I said, staring past her at the crack in the wall.

"A handsome prince, with strong arms," she said with a sly smile.

"And a gentle heart," I said, starting to thaw.

"He will run miles just to impress you and bring you the rarest flowers for your hair," Thalia said, flopping down on my bed. "You will be madly in love and live in a huge palace overflowing with princes and your people will adore you."

My mood lifted as we both giggled, imagining the gentle prince who would become my husband. I hoped she was right, but an uneasy feeling I couldn't explain gnawed at me. My thoughts kept returning to a certain amber-eyed god who made grapes in the middle of summer, and flowers bloom in darkness.

"Oh, Thalia. You have made me feel better. Thank you," I said, willing it to be true. She lightened my heart, but I was still worried. It's said that the Amazons have a rule that a girl cannot marry until she has killed an enemy in battle. I felt like I had been thrown into a fight, but I didn't know who the enemy was. Who was I to slay?

90

~ 6 ~

The next month was a buzz of activity as everyone prepared for the suitors. Servants buffed every corner of the palace to make it shine. My father, eager to show his wealth and hospitality, spared no expense. The storerooms off the west court burst with jars of oil and grains to feed the guests, and he commissioned bronze cauldrons engraved with the horns of a bull as gifts. I, however, was the fatted goat up for auction.

I trailed my mother as we planned the menu, discussed the guest list, and oversaw the preparations. Guards were always present, making it difficult to get away. However, under the guise of not feeling well, I did manage to sneak off once, but not to the sea. Instead, I slipped past the palace gates and went to Mandilari's farm. It had been several weeks since I'd seen or heard from Dionysus. When news of my wedding spread, I expected to see him. But, nothing. It was probably best since there was no future for us, but I couldn't get him out of my head. My mind kept coming back to the whisper of his lips on the back of my neck. I wanted to see him, but not at a temple. Mandilari's farm seemed like the best bet. Also, I often thought of him and his wife, and I wondered how they were doing with their farm.

As soon as they saw me, Mandilari and his wife embraced me with hugs and kisses and congratulations on my upcoming wedding. I brought her a beaded headband, which would bring out the fire in her hair. Delighted, she put it on right away and peppered me with questions about the suitors and happenings at the palace. Although I didn't want to think about my wedding, I gave her all the details. Watching the small gestures of affection pass between them made me hope that whoever was chosen for my husband would love me like Mandilari loved his wife.

Later, he showed me around the farm where his fledgling vines were indeed growing strong and would soon bear fruit. When I asked about Dionysus, he looked sympathetic. He had come by, but not recently. Shortly after our visit, and the announcement of my upcoming nuptials, Dionysus left with his followers to explore other parts of the island. My heart sank. Did he leave because of me?

When it was time to leave, Mandilari's wife pressed a small, bronze figurine of a dolphin into my hand.

"For good luck," she said, kissing me on each cheek.

Hurrying back to the palace, I tucked the dolphin into my belt, touched that she should give me something of such value when they had so little.

Since then, my days were an endless cycle of being fitted for clothes, trying on jewelry, and looking repentant under my mother's disapproving eye. Now, I had common ground with Phaedre, who watched these fittings with great enthusiasm, running her hands over the fabrics and holding them up to see which ones went best with my eyes or complemented her golden hair. We looked at brooches, glittering with jewels, and tried on headpieces to tame my hair. In those weeks leading up to the arrivals, Phaedre and I grew closer. She had a natural ability to turn clothes into outfits, and when she finished arranging me, I had to admit I felt like a bit like a swan shaking off the gangly brown feathers of youth. I started to get excited about the idea of being presented. For the first time, I had an appreciation for Phaedre. For once, we weren't rivals for our mother's attention. We were sisters.

In the beginning, I was a little nervous nobody would come. When the first ship arrived, Phaedre grabbed my hand, and we ran to the window to see who came up the road. When I learned that the first suitor was Chomius from Pylos, who was as old as my father, my heart sunk. To my relief, others followed. Guests began to pour off their ships and march up the shores, dotting the soft sand like locusts.

We dispatched Thalia to attend them and bring back information. She always came back from the guest houses armed with her impressions of the men. Thalia had a knack for impressions and capturing the essence of a person and we loved listening to her report on the strong shoulders or expert swordsmanship of the prospects.

"Kyril from the island of Andros has the smallest hands, and he waves them around as he talks like he's trying to show them off," Thalia told me one night, with an imitation that sent me into peals of laughter.

I was not to make an appearance until after the race. Before choosing a suitor, it was our custom for the unmarried girls to have a footrace to honor Hera, goddess of marriage and wives. Her blessing would guide my father's choice and make my marriage a happy one. Although I have always found this curious since her own husband, Zeus, was known for his many affairs, I didn't care. I wanted to race.

On the day of the race, the sun cooked everything in its path. Stray wildflowers poked their heads out looking for water that never came. A breeze stirred the leaves on the trees but didn't do much to cool the fifteen of us taking our places at the starting line. It should have been my friends surrounding me for this race, but after my brother, Androgeos, was killed, I was kept apart. With my new duties as the heir, I no longer had time for play, and these girls were all strangers to me. So, to celebrate my last burst of childhood, I waited silently with companions who gawked at me and preened for each other. I wished Thalia could race with me. Even Phaedre. Most of these girls were younger than me, but a few I knew. Their faces carried shadows of the young girls I once shared stories with. There was Ayia, who always cheated when we played dice, and Kyra, who's nanny made us all dolls with different colored dresses. Mine had an aqua blue dress and hair made out of the softest red thread. I looked at them now, with their angular faces and long, lean bodies and those days seemed long ago.

I waited, searching the crowd for familiar faces. My family was there and some of the suitors, along with people from town eager to celebrate my betrothal. The Priestess of Hera glided to the front and turned to address us. Her arm swept over the field in front of us.

"You will run along the edge of this field, down the hill to the stream and along the stream to the largest olive tree. From there, it's straight to the altar of Hera. The first girl to break the thread is the winner!"

The crowd clapped, cheering on their favorites. Thalia stood behind Phaedre at the sidelines, where they both beamed at me. I settled in and focused on the archer. My muscles twitched to go.

A bead of sweat rolled between my shoulder blades down my spine and settled at my belt. The archer readied an arrow and raised his bow. An imperceptible movement of his finger flung the arrow into the air. I hurled my body ahead, keeping my eyes forward like my brother had taught me. Dust flew up around me as my bare feet beat a rhythm on the baking earth. One of the younger girls ran steady in the lead, but I pumped my arms and gained on her with Kyra on my heels. We rounded the corner past the field, and my breath came fast. I kept going, trusting the strength of my burning legs. With a few strides, I was now in the front. Breathing heavy, I could hear the girls behind me, but I didn't slow down. After a while, my legs didn't burn anymore. They felt light like they were carried by Hermes' wings.

I sailed down the hill and charged toward the stream. I could feel Kyra behind me, but I pushed on to the rhythm of my breathing and my feet on the earth. I saw the gnarled trunk of the olive tree and knew I was in the final stretch. Pumping my legs harder, I charged up the hill, speeding past a young girl who was losing pace. As I sped past her, two more girls rushed up beside me. People gathered at the finish, cheering for their favorites. I could see Phaedre at the end, waving her arms, cheering for me. I gave a final push. Then, it was over. With Kyra close at my heels, I broke the thread exhausted and full of energy, proud of what my body had just done. Kyra thundered in behind me, patting my back in congratulations. The rest tumbled in after her, but it was already over. Exhilarated, I lit the flame on Hera's altar, and the Priestess invoked her blessing. With that, my girlhood was over.

After the race, servants whisked me away to get ready for the feast. To my surprise, they took me through my mother's rooms to her bathroom. Attached to her main sitting room, the bathroom was dark, softly lit by lotus-shaped wall sconces. I padded across the smooth gypsum floor and lowered myself into her clay bathtub. A servant poured warm water over me, releasing rose scented steam. I'd seen my mother in this tub hundreds of times, and it felt odd for her servants to be attending to me here, but once I sunk into the warm water, the heat melted my sore muscles, and I let it go. I closed my eyes, only to be reminded that this wasn't relaxation time. Like an army, my mother's servants filed in to wash me. One maid scrubbed and buffed my skin until it glowed, while another ripped a comb through my hair. When at last I was shiny again (and slightly red), Phaedre brought out a new gown.

"Do you like it?" Phaedre clapped, looking me over. "The color brings out the copper in your hair."

She was right. The fabric of the dress was light, like the kind my mother wore, but its bright emerald color was all my own. She slipped a gold coil bracelet onto my wrist, as the servants wound wired jewels into my hair. When they were finished, Phaedre beamed. She squeezed my hand as we walked together to the main sitting room to see our mother.

To my surprise, my father was also there. He rose when I entered and walked to meet me to take my hands in his.

"Beautiful," he said. "I cannot believe this is the same girl who used to come in muddy from running after Androgeos in the fields. Truly, you look like a princess worthy of any of these suitors." My mother nodded in agreement. I flushed at the faint approval on her face.

I bowed my head. "Thank you, Father."

"Ariadne," said my mother, "you know what is required of you."

Of course, I did. At the feast, the suitors would present themselves formally to my father. I would face them, not as a silent child, but as a princess and a woman, the prize of Crete. Since we had no male heirs, the one chosen would need to be approved by the Oracle because my husband would also be the future ruler.

We walked together as a family through the long hallways to the throne room, where we would greet the suitors. I looked over at my mother, radiant in her pale blue gown. She walked straight, her eyes forward, never wavering. She walked like a queen, never doubting that she was the most powerful woman in the room. I tried to match her confidence, but my legs shook. She squeezed my hand for a split second as we entered the throne room, which was filled with courtiers and guests. My face prickled from all the eyes on me, and I fought the urge to turn around.

My father took his seat on his alabaster throne, and my mother and I stood next to him. Since I was the one being presented, Phaedre wasn't in attendance. I guess we wouldn't want any of the suitors deciding they were bidding on the wrong princess. With a long speech, my father welcomed the guests and as he spoke about Crete's great bounty, I could feel their eyes slide over to me. I scanned the room, recognizing the familiar faces of my father's advisers and court mixed in with many unfamiliar ones, some older than me, some younger. All of them trying to study me without being obvious. Most of the surrounding islands had sent someone, usually a second son in need of a throne. All except Athens. One by one, they approached my family, where my father accepted their gifts and greeted each one.

Everything came to a halt when someone I didn't know walked in. The room stilled, holding its breath to see how he would be received. I turned to my mother, confused as to what was happening. My mother leaned over and whispered that it was Gortys, son of my uncle, King Rhadamanthus. Unlike the other guests, he was uninvited. My father's face tightened as Gortys approached, smiling like a jackal.

There are three palaces on my island, one on each end and Knossos in the middle. Each palace managed its area of the island, but from Knossos, my father ruled them all. Rhadamanthus, his younger brother, lived in Phaistos on the southern end. I heard he was popular with his people, but I had never met him. He and my father weren't close. I wondered what his son was doing here, uninvited and unannounced. Gortys had the same steely blue eyes as my father and presumably, his brother. His pointy face reminded me of an eel, with its smooth skin, small eyes, and a mouth that never closed.

After a moment of surprise, my father regained control, neutralized his expression, and extended his arms.

"Nephew," he said. "What a pleasant surprise. What brings you?"

Gortys held out an intricately carved ivory bull. "For you, Uncle. A gift from my father. He wishes to extend his suit on the fair princess."

"Rhadamanthus? A bride for himself?"

He shrugged. "Or for me. He doesn't much care which. My mother has been gone for several years. Our house lacks a woman's sensibility. A beauty such as the Princess would be much valued there. An alliance that would strengthen both our houses." He bowed to my father. A look like he'd just eaten something unpleasant came over my father's face, but he quickly stifled it. A bride for my uncle? Alarmed, I looked from my father to my mother, waiting for one of them to send my cousin on his way. My mother laid a firm hand on my arm, giving it a gentle squeeze.

"Strengthen your house, indeed," my father mumbled. He cleared his throat. "Welcome, Gortys. It is truly a pleasure to see you after all this time."

Gortys bowed again and bypassing my mother, turned to me with an oily smile. "Princess," he said, bowing deeply. I nodded in response and glanced over at my mother, gauging her reaction to this surprise guest. With one raised eyebrow, she looked through him, not acknowledging him. There was an awkward moment of silence, and then he moved on, perhaps sensing that the conversation was over. The crowd parted to allow him to pass, nobody making eye contact. He disappeared to the back of the room, while the ivory bull still sat untouched in front of my father.

The next to approach was Chomius, third son of King Neleus of Pylos. His fingers were heavy with gold rings, which would befit a king, rather than a third son. His island must be rich indeed, I thought. I nodded my head and welcomed him to our court. He quickly bypassed me to greet my father, reminding him that Pylos is a critical shipping port and a gateway of riches. With his graying, fluffy hair and sharp nose, he reminded me of a hawk caught in a windstorm. My father could have him.

Orrin, the second son of the King of Thera, introduced himself next. Unlike the others, he greeted me first before bowing to my father.

"Is it true you have a mountain of fire?" I asked him. I had heard stories of his home, where people built houses like honeycombs in the side of a mountain.

He started at my abrupt question and then grinned. "Lady, it is true. My home has many mountains, and though it has been quiet, one has spit fire." His soft brown eyes that crinkled when he smiled disarmed me, and I found myself liking him.

"That sounds dangerous," I said.

"No, no. It's perfectly safe. I would love to show you. We have many shrines to the Earth Shaker to protect us, and he has shown us favor. You would love it. The black soil gives us the sweetest grapes and wine fresh like the mountain air." After a brief pause, he added, "although the beauty of your island is remarkable as well."

"Perhaps I will see it someday," I replied, returning his smile. It was exciting to think of what lay beyond our shores.

I opened my mouth to continue, but my father stood and clasped Orrin's hands. "Orrin, welcome! Tell me news of your father. I still have the bronze javelin he gave me. Like it was forged by Hephaestus himself." As he got pulled away, Orrin gave me a sideways glance.

Before I could analyze whatever passed unspoken between us, the prince of Cythera was telling me about his strength in battle and all his riches gained from plundering the villages on the coasts of his enemies. His hands were rough, and his voice loud. While he talked to me, he looked at my mother. Many of the suitors told me of their prowess in battle, of their ships and soldiers. I wondered if they knew how many years of peace we had on Crete and if they would be content to live without battles to fight.

Demitrius, the young prince from Delos, was the last to approach. He was shorter than me and fidgeted almost as much as I did. "Princess." He bowed. "You are even more beautiful than I imagined."

I nodded my thanks and shifted in my seat. His eyes were bright green, and they seemed out of place on his round face. He appeared to be frozen.

"We are honored to have you as our guest," I said. "Please, tell me about your home." To my surprise, Demitrius did not speak of imports and exports and sources of wealth.

"It is the birthplace of light," he said grandly as if I should already know this and went on about all the ways Delos was superior.

Of course I knew that Delos was sacred because it is where Leto went to give birth to her twins, the gods Artemis and Apollo, but his smug expression annoyed me. Delos was also a stronghold of Carian pirates. It is still just as famous for pirates as it is for

Apollo. Besides, Crete has Mount Ida where Zeus was raised. My island fed and sheltered him, just as it did me. Creation is in the heart of my people. He could have his "birthplace of light." I opened my mouth to tell him so, but he cut me off with a smirk and moved on to greet my father.

That was the end of the formal greeting of the suitors. I backed up from the table feeling confused and a little overwhelmed. How could one choose a husband based on a few polite words? As my cousin pointed out, this was an alliance to be negotiated, not a marriage. I was a prize to be won, an award that carried the power of Crete. I couldn't see myself with any of these suitors with their slippery smiles and tales of war. I wondered if this is how my mother felt when she was promised to my father.

Servants ushered the guests outside to the courtyard, which had been transformed with tables, flowers, and candles for the meal. The smell of roasted lamb and goat whispered through the air while servants circled, bringing around dish after dish of olives, snails, figs, and fruit. They even carried my favorite honey cakes that I used to sneak from the kitchen when I was a child. I made a mental note to have one of the servants bring a few back to my quarters for Thalia and me to enjoy later.

The wine flowed freely, and after several amphorae had been emptied, people grew more animated. A bard wove through the courtyard with his tortoiseshell lyre singing stories of heroes and gods. Having forgotten about me, the suitors formed groups of their own, laughing and sharing stories of bloodshed and heroism, each trying to best the one next to him. I weaved among them, unable to sit still. Balen, from I forget which city, had clearly had his fill of wine. Waving his glass over his head, he told story after story of fighting and battle. With his thick back and muscled shoulders, I had no problem picturing him charging ahead through a battlefield. In fact, I couldn't imagine him doing anything else. His nostrils flared like a bull when he laughed, and he didn't notice when wine spilled, narrowly missing my dress as I tried to slip past.

I backed up right into Gortys. Startled, I jumped back.

"Careful!" he exclaimed, steadying me with a hand on the small of my back. I recoiled.

"Gortys, pardon me." I tried to turn out of his grasp, but his hand remained uncomfortably on my back.

"Are you all right? You look stricken."

I shook my head. "Yes, fine. I just need some air." I turned away, but he followed, blocking me with his body.

"What's the hurry?"

"No hurry. It's just a bit close in here."

"All of this must be a bit overwhelming for you, not used to being among all of these people."

Did he think me simple? "I'm sorry, sir. I don't catch

your meaning."

"I only meant that your father guards his jewels well."

I didn't say anything. His hand slid down to the side of my hip.

"Sir," I said, moving away. He grabbed my wrist.

"Lady. Think of what a union between our houses would bring. United power across Crete."

"That is not my decision."

"With me, you will be a queen."

"You forget yourself. I will be a queen anyway."

"I am my father's main emissary. We will see the world together."

I didn't reply.

Encouraged, he kept on. "I command my father's greatest fleet. These are times of peace. I'm sent all over to negotiate trade and breed goodwill with our allies. As my queen, where I go, you will also go. Egypt, Cypress, Palestine, Syria-all shall be yours." I tried to free myself again from him, but he tightened his grip.

"And what shall you get?" I asked.

"The envy of every man when they see the beauty and grace of my wife." His eyes swept over me, making me flinch.

I nodded my thanks at the compliment and stepped back, pulling my wrist free from him. "I thank you, Cousin, for the nice words. I really must get some air. Please excuse me." As I turned to walk away, he grabbed my arm again.

"Cousin. Think on it. Whether we do this as friends or not is up to you." He let go of my hand, and I hurried away, feeling his eyes on my back.

I ducked into one of the side porticoes to catch my breath. My heart pounded, and I needed to shake Gortys from my mind.

I stood in the dark, getting my bearings under the stars. Someone spoke, startling me. "Princess, I'm sorry to disturb." I turned around to see Orrin step out of the shadow inside the portico.

I smiled, recovering myself. "It is I who should apologize to you. It seems you were here first."

"I just needed a moment to clear my head."

"Me too."

"Then, I shall leave you," he said, starting to pass me.

"No, no. Stay. Truly. There is enough sky for both of us. Plus. I would love to hear more about your island that spits fire."

He smiled warmly, crinkling his eyes. "What would you like to know?"

"Everything."

"I will gladly tell you, but first, can I make a bold statement?"

I nodded and gestured for him to proceed.

"I saw you talking with Gortys just now. How much do you know of him?"

"Not much," I said. "He's my cousin, but this is the

first time we've met. Our fathers are not um… close."

"I thought as much. King Rhadamanthus is well-loved by his people. They praise his intelligence and honor." He stopped, looking unsure whether he should continue.

"Go on."

He took a breath. "Forgive me. Gortys does not share that reputation. He grew up spared nothing, given every indulgence. He takes what he wants with no consequences. There are many stories of… Well, I would just caution you to be careful around him."

"Thank you. I appreciate your concern and will remember your warning. But, enough of him. Orrin, tell me more about your home."

At the mention of his home, Orrin's face lit up. He spoke of his island with love, about how it barely rains and there aren't many streams, but the volcanoes heat the water underground, and they've found ways to transport it in ducts. I marveled at the idea of warm water in a bath without a fire.

As he talked, I studied him. He didn't have the brawn of the warriors, but his arms were solid. In a flash, I wondered what it would be like to have them wrapped around me, strong and safe. My face flushed at the thought, but I was saved from that rabbit hole by my mother's servant, who interrupted our conversation.

"Lady, I have been sent to fetch you. Your mother, the Queen, is retiring and she bids you to join her."

I nodded to Orrin and bid him goodnight and followed the servant through the crowd. Thalia huddled close with my father and I tried to signal to her, but she didn't see me. Or if she did, she didn't let on. I hoped she would be able to get away soon as I had much to tell her. I followed the servant back to my mother's apartments, where she was already waiting. When she saw me, she grasped my shoulders in a quick hug, brushed a stray hair out of my face and in an odd maternal gesture, kissed my forehead.

"Daughter, tonight, you made Crete proud. So many suitors. Your marriage will bring a great union," she said, still holding my hands. She was so happy and animated. We talked about the suitors and the advantages and disadvantages of each. She did not mention my uninvited cousin. He was the giant in the room that nobody spoke of. I realized, to my horror, that she leaned toward Chomius, who was nearly as old as my father. Well, not him really, but the union he would bring with the wealthy island of Pylos. Thankfully, the final say would be up to the Oracle. I said a silent prayer to the gods begging the Oracle's vision did not include me joined with an old man with fat hands and bushy eyebrows.

When my mother released me back to my room, my eyes could barely stay open. While my mind raced with thoughts of my future, my body was ready for sleep. My attendants untied my hair and helped me into my nightclothes, and I fell into bed. I tried to stay awake for Thalia, but she didn't come, and when I awoke the next morning, her bed had not been slept in.

I awoke early and threw on a modest dress, tucking the dolphin figurine into my belt. We met early, on the trail south of the palace. Although she still looked radiant, even my mother dressed in a plain tunic and wove her pale hair into a long braid down her back. Even in simple clothes, my mother could not look like anything but a queen. It was in the direct gaze of her eyes, the proud tilt of her head and the straightness of her back. She didn't worry about where she put her foot because she knew it would land on solid ground, and wherever she went, people would part for her. I wondered if when I was a queen, I would have this bearing as well.

There was no big parade. It was just my parents and

I with a few palace guards. Going to the oracle was a family matter. It was important to go on foot, to be humble in front of the gods. The air was quiet, broken only by the songs of birds chirping and the crunch of our footsteps on the path. My thoughts went to each of the suitors, wondering who would be my husband. For as long as I could remember, I had looked across the ocean and longed to see what was out there. Now, when it was in my grasp, the thought of leaving everything I knew scared me. I would be joined to one of these men. Who would it be? One of the warriors who talked of nothing except battles and glory? One of the smug princes who barely looked at me before reaching over me to my father? Orrin with his soft brown eyes and easy smile? He was the only one who didn't make my stomach knot.

My mother asked why I was so quiet. I told her that I was only nervous. I've never left our shores, and now, with a husband, I would be leaving everything I knew with someone I only just met.

She furrowed her brow. "Ariadne, you will be Queen of Crete."

"Yes, Mother. I know."

"Of Crete, Ariadne. Your husband will move here. You will teach him the ways of the island, and we will teach you both how to rule. Then, when it is time, you will take your place. You may leave to visit other places, but your home will be here." As she spoke, realization dawned. How did I not realize this? I was the heir. Something I had been training for since I was small. What an idiot I was. I thought my marriage would end like hers, with a voyage, but my future was here. How had I let myself forget that? For a moment, I thought she was going to take my hand, but she didn't.

I remained quiet as I walked steadily forward, rethinking all of my childish ideas. My marriage wouldn't be an adventure like my mother's. The furthest I would move would be to my mother's quarters, where I would come out only when needed by the king, whoever my husband was to be. This realization made my steps heavy as we moved from the road to the trails going up the mountain. The air carried the clean scent of thyme mixed with a blush of sage, and I breathed deeply, willing it to cleanse my spirit. I focused on the morning sunshine warming my skin. The higher we got, the more relaxed I became, and the sea opened up below me. From up here, it seemed endless, with the white caps of the waves kissing the shores. It reminded me of what I love about my island. If I was to be tied to a place, at least it was a place kissed with beauty. Soon, we were at the mouth of the cave. There was nobody outside.

A young girl dressed in a white tunic came out to greet us. She bowed her head before my father, took my hand, and led us into the mouth of the cave. Once we were through the opening, darkness swallowed us. After my eyes adjusted, I saw the cave opened into a larger room, lit only with a couple of lanterns. Darkness clung to the corners. I felt the closeness of the room grip me, but pushed the rising panic down. I focused on the way the candles and torches bounced light off the walls, which were slick with moisture. She left us in the middle of the cavern, and the priestess stepped forward from the shadows.

She was not what I expected. I expected someone old and gnarled, like a woman who lived in a cave. Instead, the priestess was young, with a soft, kind face. Despite the rough setting, her robes were airy and bright. She moved with a natural grace, and when she grasped my hands, I didn't feel afraid. I felt cared for. While the cave was cold, warmth radiated from her.

"Come," she said, leading me to the altar. "Bow before the Goddess."

We bowed our heads before the shrine, and my father presented offerings. At the last minute, I took the dolphin out of my belt and held it out. Now seemed like a good time for a little luck. She took the bronze figurine I offered, and turned it over in her hands before placing it on the altar next to a basin and a clay vase. She took a small jar from the altar and brought it to her lips. Like a feather floating to the ground, she knelt in front of a large covered vase. She removed the top and reached in, pulling out several wiggling, black snakes. They wound around her arms as she held them out to me. Involuntarily, I recoiled, unsure about the snakes. Their tongues flicked in and out as they wound around their priestess, but wasn't sure what I was supposed to do.

"Give me your hand," she said softly. I hesitated but obeyed.

"The temple snakes won't hurt you."

Everything else in the room faded away as the black head of the snake slid onto my palm, gliding between my thumb and forefinger and around the back of my hand. Its skin was cool and smooth as it wound around my wrist, sliding up my forearm. Another wove between my feet, its tongue flicking the instep, tasting me. For a fleeting moment, I hoped that biting me wasn't part of this ritual. The snake on my arm climbed up to my shoulder and lifted its head, bringing us eye to eye. I looked into its black face, moving back and forth, balanced in the air. It held my gaze as we studied each other, its tongue flicking in and out.

Then, its cold eyes became warm, and everything else fell away. I felt the Mother, the Goddess. She filled me with light, and the chaos inside me quieted under her gaze as warmth spread through me. In the coils of the snake around my arm, I felt her embrace, and I felt like I was laid bare. She combed through my past, my desires and my secrets. I wasn't alone. Whatever happened, with certainty, I knew I would be all right. I don't know how long we stayed like that, but in an instant, our connection was broken and the heat disappeared, replaced with the damp coolness of the cave. Once again, the snake was just a snake, gliding over my collar bone and back down my arm to the priestess.

She scooped it up, letting it crawl up her arm to her shoulder, settling around her like a shawl. She stroked its head with her finger and looked into its eyes. After a few moments, she gathered up the snakes and returned them to their basket, took another drink, and lit a candle on the altar. She lowered herself into her chair and closed her eyes. The flickering flame of the candle bounced off her face, and we sat in silence for several minutes.

"Lady," my father started, impatient. "Which of the suiters shall be her husband?"

For the first time, the priestess looked at my father. "None," she said.

"But, Chomius.." My father started.

She cut him off. "No."

I breathed a sigh of relief and fought the urge to throw my arms around her. My parents looked to each other, confused. My father started to object, but my mother laid a hand on his arm to stay him. They gestured for her to continue.

"Her path with Crete is tangled. I see a husband with great power but at a price. A sea on fire. She will hear the voiceless and unravel the strength of bulls with a thread."

I was stunned speechless. I'd never heard of the

Oracle rejecting all of the prospects. It made no sense. My head spun. I wanted to sit down, but my feet wouldn't move. At first, my father tried to argue with her. It was ridiculous. Hear the voiceless? Unravel with a thread? What did that even mean? There were princes from nearly all our allies. If none of them was suitable, who was my powerful husband to be? To my father's arguments, the Oracle simply raised her hand and said she was only the vessel. The images came from the Mother, and it wasn't for her to second guess. It was not something he could negotiate. Still. She had to be wrong. The sea on fire? Everything I love is on this island. Even if I could, I would never harm it.

We left the cave in silence and started making our way down the side of the mountain. Nobody said a word. There was an unspoken thought between us. Gortys. He had to be the cause of this. I couldn't point to why, but in my bones, I felt it was him. Orrin's words echoed in my mind. He takes what he wants. What he wanted was power. Could he be the powerful husband? Gods, I hoped not.

A little girl scurried down the hill after us. I turned to her, but my parents didn't notice. They walked ahead of me, murmuring to each other and shaking their heads, too wrapped up in their thoughts to be concerned with mine. The guards must not have thought her a threat because they didn't stop her either. She grabbed my wrist and pulled me down to her level. Her dark hair was plaited with little yellow flowers and her green eyes sparkled.

"You will go to the temple." She whispered and then turned around and ran back up the hill.

~ 8 ~

In the days that followed, Thalia and I schemed ways to sneak out of the palace. An elaborate plan grew more elaborate each day, involving creating distractions, wearing costumes, and even slipping the guards some of my mother's herbs. As it turned out, it was much easier than we thought. After we returned from the Oracle, my parents disappeared to their quarters, and the prophecy hung over the palace. It was eerily quiet. Nobody asked me to help with the weaving. I wasn't summoned to attend my mother or reminded of my chores. People looked through me, and when they spoke to me, it was with pity. I was the princess who wasn't fit to marry.

After my father announced there would be no

wedding, the suitors left one after another. All but one. Gortys stayed behind. I didn't speak with him, but I saw him walking through the courtyard and lingering in the shadows, perhaps collecting gossip to take to his father.

Orrin came looking for me, but I couldn't face him. I was too ashamed. I hid on the cliff above the bay and watched his ship sail away, back to his island that spit fire. I had plenty of time to think, and I couldn't get away from myself. I wondered what my future held. Me, the unmarriageable princess. Since I was a child, I was groomed for only one thing–to be a wife and the future of Crete. I'd failed at the one thing I was supposed to do.

If Androgeos were the heir, everything would be secure. Tall and strong, he walked with confidence like the king he was supposed to be. But, he was gone. I missed him every day, but now, the hole left by his death felt like it would swallow me.

Most people remembered him for being an athlete, winning every race, but I remembered him for the bulls. With the races, Androgeos showed off his speed, but with the bulls, he showed his heart. I loved going to the fields with him. We'd bring treats and pet the big, gentle faces of the cows and chase the calves. The bulls were kept separate, and I wasn't allowed to play with them. They were dangerous. With their sharp horns and muscled bodies, they were power. They were life. They weren't something to be pet or trifled with. Except at the spring festival.

Bull jumping at the festival was where he shined. The ring was a circle in the lower field, with onlookers all around. My brother stood in the center, all eyes on him, right where he wanted to be. He raised his arm and bowed to the rangers holding the bull. The bull stood taut at the edge, black fur shining, horns pointed forward, head aimed at the ground. Its ear twitched. Androgeos looked over at me, flashed a smile, and brought his arm down. The servant released the bull, and it charged forward. My brother dodged the pointed horns and turned to face it. The bull snorted and stomped its hoof and charged forward. Like they were dancing, Androgeos moved in time with the bull, always getting out of the way at the last second. Every time, my heart stopped. The bull twitched, Androgeos countered. The bull ran. Androgeos swerved. Around and around. Those sharp horns coming close to grazing his sides.

Finally, he moved to the back of the ring and waited, his eyes locked with the bull's. The bull kicked the ground and lurched forward, its hoofs kicking up dust as it barreled toward my bother. Instead of moving out of the way, Androgeos took the bull head-on, running towards it. The bull thundered forward, lowering its head, pointing its giant horns at my brother. Androgeos leaped at the bull, grabbing the horns. Angry, the bull howled and snapped its head back. Using the momentum, my brother vaulted backward, allowing the bull to fling him upside down, somersaulting over its back. He landed on his feet to the cheers of the crowd.

Later, when I leaped into his arms, I gripped him so tightly, not wanting to let him go. His tunic was wet, his face shiny and I breathed him in. My strong brother, who always smelt of sunshine. I felt his heart beating, strong and solid. If I had known that was the last time I would see him jump the bull, I would have held on forever and never let go. My heart still ached for him. Now, I added confusion and shame to that hole in my chest.

As Orrin's ship faded into nothing, I felt like my normal life sailed off the edge of the ocean. The hardest part was that we didn't talk about it. Even Alcina, who always had an opinion, was quiet about what the oracle said. My mother took her meals in her room alone. Maybe with my father. I don't know. Nobody said, and I didn't ask. I ate with Phaedre, mostly in silence.

So, when it was time to sneak out, I basically just left. After dinner was cleared away and shadows fell in the courtyard, I threw on a plain tunic. Alcina was busy helping my mother with something, and Phaedre was nowhere to be found. Most likely, she was with my mother, playing queen while my mother regrouped. I stole out a side door, careful to avoid the kitchen, which still bustled with servants. I crept to the road and knelt behind the big fig tree, where our hidden bundle of water skins and heavier cloaks waited. It wasn't long before I heard Thalia's light footsteps.

We set out, listening to the crunch of our feet on the path. The sun already made its way across the horizon, and the sky couldn't decide between gold and blue. We silently retraced our steps from that day we got stranded looking for herbs. Thalia was unusually quiet, and when I asked her what was wrong, she insisted everything was fine.

As we got deeper into the woods, it grew darker, but we didn't light our torches. The sky opened up into a tapestry of stars, bright and shining. Although I was nervous, the stars made me feel safe, like someone was watching out for us. We first heard drums and then laughter. The sound led us toward the cave, where grapevines now blanketed the entrance, winding up the walls and hanging down. Plump grapes spilled out on to the ground. Crumpled blankets and mats covered the floor, but the cave was empty. We went around the side to the clearing on top of the hill.

On the clearing, tall black trees formed a circle with one big tree reaching up from the center. Women wearing fawn skins danced and sang, playfully waving pine cone-tipped wands. Golden light bounced from the torches to light up their faces as they laughed together. One woman, with ivy wound through her reddish hair, seemed to float through the crowd as she swayed and waved her arms over her head. She radiated joy. After she noticed us standing there slack-jawed, she smiled a huge, toothy smile and came over.

"Ariadne, welcome," she said, bowing her beautiful head. "We knew you would come. You are welcome here in the sisterhood."

I looked down at my simple tunic, suddenly feeling very plain myself. Although I'd swear I'd never seen her before, she looked into my face like we'd known each other always. She grabbed my hand and led me to a table piled high with food and drinks and handed Thalia and I a cup of wine. As she kissed our cheeks, her warm gaze wrapped me in comfort and the part of me that had been clenched in anxiety from the Oracle relaxed.

"Come," she beckoned, leading us to the fray of dancing women. Warmed by the wine, our bodies started to feel the music. The drumbeat and the song grew louder. The strange wands made patterns in the air and energy vibrated all around us. My feet moved in rhythm with the wands, and next to me, Thalia closed her eyes. We bounced and twirled together, and the sweet voices of the women's song melted the air around us. When our cup was empty, another appeared.

I closed my eyes and let the music run through me, the rhythm beating in my chest. Then, his world opened up to me. I saw baby Dionysus splashing in the water at Nysa, the rain nymphs taking care of him. Then, as he grew, the pain of belonging to neither the mortal world nor to Mt. Olympus. I felt his joy when he crushed the grapes and mixed them with the fermented honey, instinctively knowing what to do to create something new. Always running. Always hiding from Hera, who chased him still, punishing him for his mother's transgressions.

I felt untethered. My heart was light, but my mind returned when the prickle of someone watching me crept up my neck.

"You are beautiful when you dance."

I turned to look into the amber eyes of the god himself, like fire barely contained. Dionysus. I felt him in my stomach, and my breath caught in my throat.

"You came," he said.

Again, I bowed my head. "Of course."

"Welcome, Princess. My temple has no walls. It's the air we breathe and the wine we drink. It's all around us and everywhere." The other women also noticed his presence and were drawn to him, sashaying past him, trying to get close to him. He brushed off each one and never looked away from me. My stomach flopped, and my face flushed red. I took another sip, and warmth spread through my veins.

One of the women, beautiful in her fawn skin clothing and bright blond hair, glided toward him, snaking her arm around his waist and put her lips near his ear and whispered something I couldn't hear. Uncomfortable, I patted my wild hair, which had escaped the confines of the plait, and wished I possessed such confidence and grace. He brushed her off and she glided off, returning to the group of women, who enfolded her into their dance. He watched them for a moment and then turned back to me.

"The night has just begun. Come. Enjoy. Become one with the fruit that the land provides, my beautiful..." Then, he disappeared into the crowd.

Thalia's eyes were huge. I took her hand, and like a dream, we floated light and happy, enveloped back into the group, swaying and dancing. The wine continued to flow into my glass, and when I looked at Thalia, her face was bright. I grinned back at her. The woods blurred into the background. The drum beat into my chest. I was sweaty and laughing and happy. Joy hung in the air like the fragrance of grapes.

After a while, we fell exhausted onto a patch of soft grass. As we lay catching our breath, we began to notice that the dancing had gotten faster and more frantic. The women shook their hair and roared, almost a primal scream. Some bared their teeth. The air shifted from joy to something else. The torchlight bounced off them, but instead of making their faces glow, it accentuated their shadows, making them frightening. Frenzied energy crackled around us. I looked over to see Dionysus standing on the edge, calmly watching the women. He looked over at me, and his smile shot warmth into the pit of my stomach.

Then, the main priestess led a small goat into the fray. His fur was white like clouds, and his eyes darted around, unsure of what was happening. They chanted and sang a song of blood and death, of the earth ripping the vines apart.

They descended on the goat, tearing and clawing at it. It bleated in panic and then we couldn't see it anymore. Panting and savage, the women came up for air with blood on their hands and around their mouths. Their eyes were wildfire.

Like a spell broken, I crashed back to myself, grabbed Thalia's hand, and ran.

We didn't think. We didn't talk. We ran, swift and fast like a deer away from the cave. Away from the women. Away from the horror and their bloody faces. We only stopped once, when the bile had risen so far in my throat that I had to stop and throw up.

~ 9 ~

The light streaming in from the window stabbed me awake. Was morning always so bright? My head hurt. When I moved, searing blows like my brain scraping on the inside of my skull combined with a feeling that the room was a little off-kilter. On her cot next to me, Thalia had one eye open, wincing at the sunlight. I forced myself to sit up, sure of only one thing. I needed water. Lots of water. I pushed myself up to standing and held out my hand to Thalia. She took it, and with a collective groan, we started our day.

After getting dressed, Thalia lumbered off to start on her chores, and I sat alone for several moments, going over the events of the previous night. Fuzzy images of dancing and Dionysus. The goat. The blood. It seemed surreal. A proper sacrifice had ritual and respect. There was no divine in what we saw, only drunken savagery. Hurt and shock fought each other in my mind, leaving behind a blanket of numbness.

I wanted to talk about it, but I didn't have the words. What was there to say? What bothered me the most is the memory of his face at Mandilari's farm, bursting with pride. He wanted to help the most impoverished farmer. Was I wrong to see good in him? He wanted me to come to his temple. For what? To join his pack of followers? To show me what he was? I didn't understand how the god I thought I glimpsed could be the same one who instigated such frenzy. I rubbed my temples and flopped back down on the bed, burying my head under a blanket.

In the next few days, I barely saw Thalia, and she often didn't come back to our room at night. I wondered what was keeping her, thinking she was probably hiding away with Darius. I hoped she wasn't avoiding me because of what happened at the cave. Grapevines sprung up everywhere, up the window in my room, around the entrance of the labyrinth, around the chair where I ate breakfast. I tore all of them down and had the servants burn them. It was risky to provoke his anger, but I didn't care. I couldn't see them without seeing the terrified eyes of the goat and the blood around the women's mouths. Besides, deep down, I still wasn't afraid of him. I was angry at him.

I was a ghost in the palace. Except to feed Asterion, I wasn't asked to do anything. With my new found freedom, I did what I pleased. I ran along the shore and gathered plants for my mother, careful to avoid the area around the cave. I gave flowers and herbs to her as a kind of peace offering, and although she accepted them politely, they didn't bring peace. It was as if she didn't know what to do with me. So, as her attention turned to Phaedre, the two of them became inseparable. From the sidelines, I watched my mother and Phaedre, heads bent together, with a pang because that common ground I found earlier with Phaedre was gone. With Thalia being busy and my mother and Phaedre in their own bubble, it was lonely. To escape, I sought out the sea.

I perched on the edge of the cliff and watched the boats come in, wondering what and who they brought. I didn't sneak off to the marketplace. Instead, I grabbed my plain tunic and marched into it, daring the people I came across to question where I was going. Nobody asked. At the marketplace, I bought Phaedre a hair comb that matched the color of her eyes and some of Thalia's favorite cheese. I hoped these offerings would create a bridge. Mostly, I just walked. And listened. And breathed. The talk of the marketplace was Theseus, the hero from Athens. Stories of his Herculean feats were thrown about from stall to stall, growing in magnitude with each telling.

"That club was made by Hephaestus himself. You can't break it. Nobody could get it off of that nasty Cyclops until Theseus came along. He tells the Cyclops he doesn't believe his club is really bronze. Can you believe that? Says it's just painted to look that way."

The leatherworker chuckled, shaking his head. "Only Theseus would say that to a Cyclops."

"They argued about it for hours, and finally, he hands it over so Theseus could inspect it. Well, he inspected it all right. Took that club and bashed his head right in."

It seems like everywhere I went, people competed with each other over who had the greater tale of Theseus' bravery. Stories of how he cleared the land of bandits and one that made me stop in my tracks- how he slayed the white bull that sired Asterion.

Through the years, many people had gone after that bull and failed. If he succeeded, Theseus must be a warrior indeed. I walked through the marketplace, looking at the trinkets laid out on blankets and and listening to life bustle all around me. I wondered what was happening in the cave near the cliff in the woods, and I worried about what my future held. As I tried to shake these thoughts, I started to feel conscious of my footsteps. The sense that I was being watched crept up the back of my neck. I shrugged it off at first and tried to ignore it, telling myself I was being foolish, that I had an overactive imagination. I pushed forward, switched direction, and ducked behind a tapestry, but the feeling intensified.

The light had turned soft as it does right before day turns to night and I realized it was later than I thought. I needed to get out of here. I hurried back down the road to the palace, suddenly conscious that I was alone on the road. It was then that the prickle of fear turned to dread. There was someone behind me.

I sped up. So did the footsteps. They got faster and closer. I started to run. Heart thumping, I bolted for the stables. They weren't far, and I knew that if I made it there, I would find Darius.

My feet pounded the ground, but I wasn't fast enough. Someone grabbed my arm. I spun around into the slippery, grinning face of my cousin, Gortys. His smile slid over me like an eel.

"Cousin. Why are you running from me? I thought we could walk together."

"Release me," I said, trying to push down my fear.

"We're family. You have nothing to fear from me."

"Glad to hear it. Again. Release me."

"Sadly, I cannot. You are to be my wife. After that, you may do what you please." His fingers dug into my arm.

"Your wife? No. Haven't you heard? The Oracle said that my husband hasn't arrived yet."

"The Oracle is wrong. You will be my wife, and we will unite Crete."

I pulled, trying to free my arm from his grasp, but

he tightened it.

I yelped in pain.

"Stop struggling, and it won't hurt… As much." He chuckled.

"You are repugnant. Let me go!" I swung my free arm at him, but he caught it easily and leaned in close. His fetid breath brushed my cheek.

"Stupid girl."

His other hand moved to my leg, pushing up the outside of my thigh. He licked his lips. "You are my birthright. Don't worry. I'll put a prince in here," he said, moving his hand up to my belly.

A scream got stuck in my thought as I started shaking and twisting, trying to get away. He overpowered me. Panic rolled over me in waves, but I couldn't think. This was it. This was the prophecy. If he succeeded and married me by force, there would be civil war. My father's pride would not let this insult stand. He would go to war with his brothers. In my terror, I could see it clearly. Ships burning to ash in the harbor. Just like the Oracle said, I was to be the instrument of Crete's ruin. Gods help me. I started to cry, which made Gortys smile.

He laughed at my weakness as he leered closer. "Don't cry, Princess. You might find you like it."

I felt something harden in me. I screamed as loud as I could and brought my heel down on the top of his foot. He shouted in pain and slapped my face hard with the back of his hand. My head whipped back, and I fell to the ground. The blood tasted metallic in my mouth. My cheek throbbed. My resolve hardened. I didn't care what happened to me. I wasn't leaving with him.

I scooted backward away from him and tried to scramble to my feet, but he pushed me back down and stood looming over me. Still smiling, he bent over me. I looked up into his disgusting eyes, took a deep breath, and screamed. Startled, he recoiled. Seeing my opportunity, I kicked him hard between the legs. He clutched himself and dropped over to the side, making a satisfying squeaky gasping sound.

I scrambled backwards to my feet and ran. Heart thumping, I sprinted toward the stables, frantic for anyone who could help me.

Up ahead, I spotted a familiar figure further up the road. His rolling gate was unmistakable, and I yelled out to him. Darius.

When he recognized me, a smile brightened his face but then turned to concern as he registered my panic. For a moment, he was the boy I knew. My friend.

"Lady, what's the matter? What happened?" His formal tone hurt more than the mark on my face.

"Darius, please," I said, wanting my old friend back. I told him what happened, what Gortys had done. He took in my face, my clothes. I told him I needed to get back to the palace. Nobody knew where I was.

He took my hand. His hand was rough and solid. Safe. "He will not hurt you. I promise."

Darius and I rushed to the stables, where I collapsed on a hay bale. My legs felt wobbly and I needed to catch my breath. I don't think he knew what to say, so he didn't say anything. He just sat next to me until I was ready to go. When I was ready, he picked up an ax from the corner and we started down the trail to the palace. As weapons went, an ax was not ideal, but it was something and I was relieved to have his company. There was no sign of Gortys. Perhaps he saw his plan failed and ran away. Or, I worried that maybe he waited for me closer to the palace.

We walked on, but Gortys didn't return. Feeling the immediate danger had passed, our walk slowed to a normal pace, and we relaxed a bit. We walked in silence, our footsteps falling in sync.

"Lady," he said, looking down and out of the corner of his eye.

"Yes?"

"Maybe I shouldn't ask, but... what of Thalia?"

"What do you mean?"

He kicked the dirt at his feet. "I haven't seen her lately. She hasn't asked me to accompany her to the market, and she hasn't stopped by the stables. Is she all right?"

"What do you mean? I know she's been sneaking off at night to see you. Don't worry. I'm not mad, and I won't tell." Why would he pretend otherwise? I didn't understand what he was getting at.

Now, he looked confused as well. "No, lady. I

swear. She hasn't. I haven't seen her for several days. Or nights."

"What?" I said, confused. I stopped to face him. "You haven't seen her at all?"

He shook his head. "No, not in several days."

Worry bit into my chest, but I forced a reassuring smile. "Well, I'm sure her duties have kept her very busy lately. It's nothing to be concerned about." If she hasn't been with Darius and she hasn't been in our room, where has she been?

"I suppose you're right," he said, but he didn't sound convinced.

When we were almost to the palace, Darius stopped and darted into the brush on the side of the road. He came out holding a handful of flowers, their yellow centers bright against the delicate, white petals.

"Thalia loves these. She says they smell like autumn. Here. Smell," he said, holding it out to me.

"She's right. They do." I agreed.

"Can you give these to her? In case she's mad," he asked.

"I'm sure she's not, but of course, I will." I took the flowers, and we walked the rest of the way in silence. I thanked him for escorting me home. Once inside, I needed a moment to myself. My thoughts were reeling. I headed to my room, thinking I could delay a few minutes dropping off the flowers before finding my father.

My parents saved me the trouble. When I got to my

room, they were waiting for me, looking stern. My father stood with his arms crossed while my mother paced back and forth, and Alcina was nowhere to be found.

Despite my mother stony expression, I wanted to fly into her arms, to safety. Instead, I straightened my back and made my expression neutral, like I'd been taught.

"Mother. Father," I said, bowing to each one.

"I won't ask where you've been," my father said. "It doesn't matter." My mother laid a hand on his arm.

"Father," I interrupted, breaking into tears. I didn't want to hear another speech about sneaking out, and I couldn't hold it in anymore. The story of what happened on the road and how Darius had taken me home tumbled out of me.

As I talked, my father hardened, and my mother softened. She put her arm around me and smoothed my hair. With a crack, my father's fist pounded the wall behind him.

"That demon! I will have every sentry out looking for him. This insult will not stand. He will pay. My brother will pay."

"No," I cried. "This is the prophecy. If you go to war, it will come true."

"She's right," my mother said. "He must be dealt with, but it requires a more subtle hand. Find him. Keep him. I will handle it."

A look of admiration passed between my parents.

My father nodded his assent.

"Ariadne," my mother started. "About the prophesy." Something about her tone made my heart sink.

"I know Gortys is the destruction the oracle warned about. I know it." I looked from parent to parent, pleading for their agreement.

"We don't know that. We have to protect Crete, whatever the cost," my mother continued.

"Of course," I said, searching their faces for a hint.

"I know you love our island, sweet," my father said.

Bile threatened to rise up my throat. "Father, I would never…"

He held up his hand. "Please. Let me finish. The Oracle made me realize that we cannot put Crete at risk by choosing poorly for you. Princes and potential husbands came from all of our allies to ask for your hand. Good men. Yet, none were suitable. The Oracle has never before refused a match."

I nodded, with a pang remembering Orrin and my imagined adventure on his island with the houses in the mountain. Although it was only a week or so ago, it seemed like the life of another girl.

He continued. "Before all of this with Gortys, we made a decision, which is why we were waiting for you." He paused. My stomach clenched. "Now, it's probably more important than ever. We've decided, Ariadne, that you shall not marry. The Oracle saw a powerful husband for you, one that hasn't yet presented himself. One that could be our ruin. We can't risk that. We need to protect you and so protect Crete. So, you are to remain on the palace grounds. No more sneaking off."

The air sucked out of my body. Speechless and a little dizzy, I crumpled to the floor in shock. The only paths available for girls were to become wives or priestess and I'd only ever been trained for marriage. Not that I was in a hurry to be wed, but with a husband, I would have more freedom. I'd be my own woman, in charge of my own household. As Gortys so aptly pointed out, when my husband visits neighboring islands, I could go as well. For me, marriage was the only way. With that off the table, I'd be forever confined to these walls. Each day would be the same as the one before it. Like blowing out a candle, my world went dark.

Now, my mother spoke, trying to make her voice gentle. "I know you are upset. Think about it. It's really the best thing. You will be safe here. Maybe, after a while… " Her voice trailed off.

With that, they turned and walked out, leaving me on the floor. The tears rolled down my face. I didn't try to stop them. Alcina came in quietly and picked me up off the floor. I fell limp into her arms like a piece of seaweed and sobbed until I had no more tears to cry. She didn't say anything. She held me and rubbed my back and brushed the hair out of my eyes.

The next morning, grapevines grew up the wall and

139

around the window. I tore them down. I'd had enough of gods and prophecies.

SHIP 2

~ 10 ~

As promised, my father sent his soldiers after Gortys. Until he was found, guards followed me everywhere. Confined to the palace walls, I spent most of my days quietly weaving or sewing with Phaedre and my mother. The days got long. Under all of this protection, I was starting to get twitchy. Even at night, I couldn't escape them. The guards stood outside my room as I slept.

Since I was a child, I chased my mother's approval, which always hung just out of reach. Now, after the Gortys incident, she was affectionate. Twice, she kissed me on the forehead. However, when I asked her questions about Gortys or my future, she always changed the subject. She said I was to be patient, and it would resolve itself. I tried. We sat together, Phaedre and my mother and I. Minutes stretched into hours which stretched into what seemed like an eternity. I hated sewing. With weaving and spinning, I could find a rhythm, but sewing eluded me. My stitches were jagged and uneven, my lines not straight. I often had to rip out stitches and try again.

Frustrated, I put my project down and stood up. I had to stretch and move. My mother got up and joined me.

"Don't worry. They will find him," she said, putting her hand on my shoulder.

I nodded in agreement, but I wasn't thinking about Gortys. She thought I was restless because I was afraid. However, it was the opposite. I was restless because I wasn't afraid. I felt trapped. Because of his heroic actions, Darius was given a reward and permission to marry. While I was happy for him and excited for what that meant for Thalia, I knew the truth. Darius didn't save me. I saved myself. The worst happened. When Gortys attacked me, he thought it would be easy. That I wouldn't fight back. The memory of it choked me. But, he ended up on the ground because I put him there. When there was nobody to save me, I saved myself. Before, I didn't know I could. Now, I did.

As a reward, I felt like a prisoner, locked up for my own good. I sewed, and I wove, and I looked at everyone's concerned faces, and I waited.

143

It was a few days before the guards came back dragging a dirty, bedraggled Gortys behind them. I was sewing with Phaedre when the news rippled through the palace. My parents never announced what he had done, but rumors always circulate and when a noble is brought forth in chains, people notice. Everyone came out to the courtyard to take a look. I didn't want to go. I didn't want to look at his repulsive face or hear his justifications for what he had done, but I had no choice.

Phaedre grabbed my hand, and we went together to the courtyard, where my father waited. Gortys was brought forward alone in shackles between two guards. His men were locked away. The guards threw him before my father, and he fell to his knees. Even then, as my father looked down on him with scorn, his face held an expression of defiance.

"Gortys. Your behavior grieves me. You have brought shame to your father and our family," my father said as if addressing a misbehaving child.

"Sir, I have not. I only seek what is mine." Gortys replied.

"You mean, what is MINE," my father thundered, his eyes blazing.

Gortys shrunk back, not used to seeing my father's fury. My father held his ground.

"Still," my father continued, steadying himself. "I have no quarrel with your father. I don't wish to fight with him or you, nephew. After all, I remember when you were born." He paused and took a breath, put his hand on Gortys shoulder. "Our family has lost too many sons already." I stiffened. Where was the justice? The punishment?

Gortys brightened. "It wasn't my wish to harm you, my King, or your beautiful daughter."

"Yes. Well, we are family. Let's move past it. Come inside, and we will speak of an alliance between our great houses." He clasped Gortys by the hand and pulled him up to standing. My mind raced. What was happening? They walked inside, my mother trailing behind them. Phaedre and I started to follow, but my mother halted us with her hand. Alcina took us back to our quarters.

Later, two guards escorted Gortys out of the palace. While his men and a crowd of people watched, he hugged my father as any doting nephew and gave his regards to my mother. He lingered in front of me, but instead of an apology, he winked at me. It took every bit of self-control I had not to fling myself at him fists first. Instead, I made my face blank and didn't acknowledge him. I wanted him to know that to me, he was nothing. My father bid him a safe journey and asked to bring his goodwill back to his father, with the news of the renewed relationship between our two families.

I was shaking with something that was either fury or fear. I hoped I wasn't an olive branch to be dangled in front of my uncle to bring about this "renewed relationship." My family stood and watched as his procession disappeared over the bridge and faded onto the road heading away from the palace. When he was out of sight, my father turned to my mother.

"It is at least a twelve hour journey back to Phaistos."

My mother nodded. "The tincture I gave him will work in six. He will be well away from the palace."

"There is no trace?"

"None."

"Good." My father nodded, took my mother's hand, and led us back to the palace. My legs felt wobbly. I should have felt relief, maybe happiness that he was gone. I didn't. Fear prickled down my back, along with the unshakable feeling of dread of how my uncle would react.

"Come, Ariadne. It is over," she said as we walked back to the palace.

* * *

It was over, but it wasn't all right. I was restless and still trapped in the palace, back in the routine of sewing, and weaving like nothing had happened. After Gortys left, the guards eased up, but everywhere I went, eyes followed me with sideways looks of pity and concern. It was stifling. Even though Gortys had done something horrible to me, I couldn't shake the feeling that it was somehow my fault, like I had somehow provoked him and caused this mess. If my uncle declared war, it would be my fault.

I was also missing Thalia. While I was confined with my mother and Phaedre, Alcina kept Thalia busy. Just as my mother taught me how to run a household, Alcina showed Thalia how to manage the servants. Not that I was getting married anytime soon, but if I did, Thalia would come with me. I guess Alcina thought it was better to be prepared. Even when we were together during the day, she seemed to always find an excuse to hurry off. At night, she either crept in while I was asleep or not at all. More and more, I woke up alone in my room. I wondered where she was at night, and I couldn't shake the feeling that she was avoiding me. I started to get short-tempered, lashing out at nothing, feeling trapped. I needed to get out in the open air.

My opportunity came about a week later in the form of an envoy from my uncle in Phaistos. He sent his son-in-law, Calix, with the sad news that Gortys died on the journey home. Naturally, we met him with tears and expressions of disbelief, which he received graciously. My stomach clenched as I expressed my condolences. Not wanting him to get any ideas about whisking me away to Phaistos, my mother sent me away from the palace on an errand.

I bolted back to my room, in an un-princess-like manner, one I was glad Phaedre didn't witness. Disappointed that Thalia was nowhere to be found, I

147

took two guards and headed off to the woods to look for dittany for my mother. She claimed she needed it urgently, but the night we got stranded, Thalia and I filled an entire basket. Also, it wasn't in season. I suspected my mother picked that plant because it was elusive and grew the farthest from the palace. Finding it now would be difficult. However, I was not one to turn down an afternoon outdoors away from the palace, and I didn't argue.

Despite being in its final throes, summer would not let go. The air was hot and dry, and the sun was a balm to my spirit. Just feeling it brought a smile to my face. The ground was dusty, and the occasional gust of wind whipped the dirt into clouds, leaving my face and hair grimy. The guards trailed behind me, grumbling and sweaty. It was a relief to get under the canopy of the trees, but it wasn't much cooler. We trudged on in silence, as I searched the rock faces for the elusive small, fuzzy leaves and delicate pink flowers. The guards kept a respectful distance, not speaking to me and barely to each other. Their silence made me miss Thalia and our games, which would make this outing more fun. Still, it was a relief to be out of the weaving room, and we kept on, only stopping at a stream to refill our water skins.

As we got closer to where Dionysus made his temple, we heard angry voices coming from the direction of the cave. My head jerked up when a woman screamed, and without thinking, I bounded up the trail. The guards scrambled after me. Outside the cave, a group formed, women on one side, men on the other, like the start of a boxing match. I recognized the women from the temple; they still wore their fawn skins over their dresses and their hair loose and wild. In the warm sunlight, the priestess' red hair glowed like a flame, and the look on her face matched it. A large man with a shaggy black beard gripped a tiny woman by the arm and was trying to drag her away from the group. His face was scrunched and angry. The priestess blocked the way.

"You will not take her," she said, planting her feet.

"She's my wife. She will come home," he growled, eyes blazing.

The woman looked between them, limp and afraid. He gripped her arm tight, in a way that reminded me of Gortys. He had the same self-satisfied look on his face, which prickled up the back of my neck.

"Let go of her," I yelled as I stepped into the clearing.

At the sound of my voice, everyone snapped out of their standoff and turned to stare first at me and then at the guards shuffling up behind me.

"Lady," the man said, bowing his head. "This is none of your concern. You best keep moving."

"What is going on here?" I demanded, straightening myself up to my full height and assuming the posture I'd seen my mother make a hundred times.

Nobody spoke. "Well," I said. "Answer me. What's

going on here?" Behind me, I heard one of the guards unsheathe his sword. The air around us stilled.

"Lady," the man started again, "this is not your concern. I'm merely taking back what's mine." He didn't let go of the woman, who had shrunk back and studied her feet. He gestured behind him, where his men parted to show a man in chains. I gasped. Although he wore a simple tunic, his face was unmistakable. Dionysus.

"This fraud," the man continued, sweeping his arm toward Dionysus, who suppressed a smile, "has taken my wife-all these women. Against their will. Turned them into savages." He spit the word, looking at Dionysus with disgust. Remembering the wine-fueled frenzy at the top of the hill, I flinched, wondering if his claim had merit, but I kept on.

My heart slammed in my chest, and I struggled to keep my voice calm. "These women don't look held against their will." I turned to the priestess. "Have you been kidnapped?"

She laughed. "Of course not. We are here on our own and follow where the god leads. He hasn't kidnapped us. He has freed us." With a contemptuous glance at the man, she added. "If his wife has fled, perhaps she had nothing to stay for." She laughed again, raking her gaze suggestively over the husband. The women behind her twittered, as if at an inside joke. The woman in question shrunk even further, getting smaller by the moment.

"God?" The man replied, incredulous. "He is no god! His mother was mortal. He is a charlatan. A man pretending to be a god. He has tricked these women." At this, Dionysus stiffened but kept his placid expression.

This could not end well. He was a fool to think he had the upper hand with a god in chains, even if he only believed him a partial god. Pentheus probably thought the same, right before he was ripped apart.

The man continued, "He forces them to run off, to shame themselves. It's over now. We're taking them back." He gestured to his friends, who all grumbled their agreement.

At any moment, Dionysus could have easily freed himself from the chains binding his wrists and ended this disagreement. Why hadn't he? The fact that he found himself in chains at all was curious. Of all of the people gathered by the cave, he was the only one who was not angry, and I searched his face for a clue. I found nothing other than a raised eyebrow and a slight half-smile. He was having fun.

The man's wife looked up at her husband, eyes pleading. "Stop it, Sander. You don't know what you are doing. Please, just go home. I have not been tricked." He didn't budge.

The Priestess stepped forward. "This god is unlike others. He teaches men. He doesn't subdue them. People are fed and happy. Because of him."

His wife continued, "Please, just go home. Leave

151

me. There is nothing left ..." Her voice trailed off, and she dropped at his feet. As she crumbled, he puffed up his chest.

"You are coming home," he bellowed. At his raised voice, I flinched and glanced over at Dionysus. His eyes narrowed, but he didn't move.

"No," his wife said, yanking her arm, but he didn't let go. Angry now, the back of his free hand smacked her face, causing her to fall to the ground. Crumpled and shaking, I could see she was crying. Women ran out and gathered around her, trying to shield her with their bodies.

"Enough!" I yelled. For a moment, everything went quiet. I straightened, willing myself taller.

"I am Ariadne, daughter of King Minos and Queen Pasiphae." The guards behind me stepped forward, their hands ready on the hilt of their swords. I may have been disheveled, but the guards looked every inch the royal protectors they were.

The man dropped his wife's arm. "Princess," he said, bowing down.

"Quiet," I said. My pulse raced. I didn't know what I was going to say, but I had their attention. I looked to Dionysus, who was now grinning at me.

"Look at these women," I began, gesturing to the women huddled around the wife. "If they look distressed, it's not due to this new god. They've told you as much. It's you that does not belong here. Lady," I said, indicating the priestess. "Why do you follow this new god?"

She stood up and turned toward me. "Why? Because he is not like the others. He is not outside of us. He is one of us. He makes us more of ourselves, fills us with courage and merriment. His bounty spreads with the vine across countries."

"These men say he has tricked you, that the rites are wild and uninhibited, unnatural," I said, remembering the goat. Did the husband say unnatural? Well, maybe I added that last bit, but I wanted to hear her response.

"Unnatural? What's unnatural about living with joy? We are not harming anybody."

Again, the image of the white goat and the blood around their mouths jumped into my mind. "Do the rituals not get somewhat… um… savage? " I asked, more for myself than the men in front of me. I started to shift on my feet and then caught myself and stood firm, making my face hard again.

"Not savage, Lady. Powerful. Think of the vine. They bear tremendous fruit, life-giving fruit. Then, we prune the branches, cut them back, leaving only the bare branch. In winter, it's an old, gnarled stump and you wonder if it will ever bear fruit again. But it does. It's torn to pieces, but it puts itself back together. It comes back. In spring, the leaves grow fresh and start again. There is beauty and balance in that rendering. In him as well. It's not savage. It's nature." She said, her voice gentle.

"And you?" I asked, indicating the wife, still on the ground looking up at me. "Are you here of your own desires? Did you leave your husband to follow this new god?"

She nodded. "Yes, Lady. When I saw him, I knew it was the gods' will that I help spread his message."

"And you wish to stay?"

"Yes, Lady."

"Do you have children?"

"No, lady. We had a daughter... but she died."

I nodded at her and tried to keep my face blank. After seeing her brute of a husband, I could imagine well enough what life she left behind.

"Well, it doesn't seem that this woman was coerced." I glanced over at the woman, who was still on the ground, cupping her cheek. "Regardless of what they do, I would say that she is safer here with these women than she is with you. The only violence I've seen here today has been from you. I would recommend you take your men and return home and leave her be."

"Lady, she is my wife. By Grecian law, she is mine to do with-"

"Sir." I interrupted him. "You are not in Greece. You are on Crete. I would say again that you should return home and leave her be."

If my guards were not at the ready, I can't say what he would have done. The hatred on his face startled me. Nobody had ever looked at me that way.

However, thankfully, the guards were there, swords ready. Overhead, the wind rustled the leaves and brushed my skin. The air moved again. I don't know what my father would have done, but I suspect my mother would have sided with the women and in my heart, I knew it to be the right thing. Whatever happened in their nighttime rituals, she was there of her own choice. Who was I to take that choice away from her?

The man looked from me to his wife and over to Dionysus, who cocked his head and lifted his eyebrows. Nobody moved for several moments and then the man turned with a huff and retreated, stomping past the guards and almost knocking me over. As soon as he was gone, the chains binding Dionysus fell to his feet, and he stepped free. The men holding him quickly scurried like rats down the path after their friend. The man's wife let out a huge breath and rose to her feet, shaky and teary. She reached for her friends, who gathered her into their circle. They locked together, comforting each other.

"Princess, that was magnificent! I knew you had that in you." Dionysus started, beaming at me.

"You!" I yelled, forgetting myself. Something about his smug, lopsided smile set me off. "This is not a game. You just stood there and let them tie you up. Would you have let him take her, this girl who left her family to follow you?" I was incredulous.

Startled by my anger, Dionysus now looked

sheepish. I suspect it had been a while, if ever, since someone spoke frankly with him. I didn't care. Perhaps, after my encounter with Gortsy, I was a little sensitive about a woman being forced down a path she didn't choose, but it enraged me that he hadn't taken that woman's fate seriously. Or his own, for that matter. It was foolish of those men to challenge him and try to put him in chains, but stories spread like wildfire through the towns. If he wanted to be accepted and loved, he needed to stand up for the people closest to him. If these women were his family, he needed to protect them.

"My Princess. Of course not. Maybe I got caught up in the excitement…."

"These women trust you. They left their families for you. They all rose to defend and protect you even as you just stood there and let them get attacked. You were supposed to be better than that."

His face was soft, his eyes down. Somehow this infuriated me more. I glowered at him, wanting to punch him right in his self-satisfied smile. His followers, still holding each other, stared. I had no more words. I turned and stormed down the path with the guards trailing after me.

I had a long walk home to sort through my feelings and calm down. I couldn't believe what I had just done. My hands were trembling, but I felt almost giddy. In the end, we returned home in failure, not having gotten the dittany for my mother. She didn't

156

seem to mind, though or even notice. Her energy was focused on the upcoming dinner with Calix, no doubt wondering why my uncle sent him and what he wanted.

My mother frowned when she saw my disheveled appearance, and I was sent to be scrubbed and polished. I was thrilled to see Thalia waiting for me in my room, bringing steaming water from the fire to the basin. Humming with excitement over what happened, I ran to her, spilling out the scene in the forest. When I saw her face, I stopped. Her brow was furrowed and her eyes blank, looking past me. Noticing that I was studying her, Thalia unhunched her shoulders and wiped her nose. A mask of politeness settled over her features. Something was wrong.

"Thalia, is everything all right?"

"Yes, yes. Fine. Just tired. Come. You need to get dressed."

She brushed me away and picked up the outfit my mother laid out for me. It was a pale yellow beaded dress, serviceable and not revealing in any way. I guess my mother didn't want Calix getting any ideas. After helping me clean up and get dressed, Thalia finished by carefully winding golden ivy leaves through my hair. With the forest washed off and my hair tamed, I felt better, but I was worried about Thalia. She brushed me off and pushed me out the door to the dining area to entertain our guest.

Dinner was a simple one. We were seated at a long table laden with bowls of olives and figs along with barley bread and goat cheese. My mother, Phaedre, and I sat rigid on one side, waiting for my father and Calix. I wondered what news he brought from my uncle, King Rhadamanthus.

My father and Calix walked in arm in arm, casually laughing like old friends over a shared joke. Earlier in the day, they went out hunting together and killed the boar that would serve as the centerpiece of our meal. As much as I didn't want to be sitting here, I had to admit that it smelled divine. They took turns telling us about the hunt, each interrupting the other to add flavor to the story. My mother looked on with interest, asking questions where appropriate and congratulating them on their success. Phaedre and I listened quietly. In truth, I was only half listening. The figs were plump and ripe, and most of my attention went to enjoying their soft, sticky sweetness, like eating a flower. Next to me, Phaedre was equally absorbed, sticking goat cheese into her figs and popping them in her mouth. Given the circumstances surrounding the last visitor from Phaistos, I found my father's embracing of Calix odd and somewhat unsettling.

The servants brought out the boar, which looked as good as it smelled. Dinner carried on with my mother not speaking while Phaedre and I awkwardly responded to questions when asked. We were all in the background, an audience to my father and Calix's stories. My mother inquired after Calix's wife, my cousin. When he spoke of his wife, his face lit up. He told us stories of his young son, who loved getting into mischief and loving anecdotes of his little family. As he spoke, I studied him. His face was open, with a long nose and an easy smile. Unlike Gortys, his smiles were genuine. I started to relax a little. Suddenly, my father stood up and raised his glass of wine.

"To Gortys," he beamed. "My nephew. Gone too soon. May he have eternal peace and glory in the underworld."

Calix raised his glass as well, and my mother smiled brightly and shot Phaedre and me a look. On cue, I smiled, raised my cup, and bent my head to honor my cousin, who tried to abduct me and who my mother had poisoned.

"To the ongoing love and partnership between Knossos and Phaistos," Calix said, holding his glass and tipping his head toward my father. My father raised his glass in return. A long silence followed before Calix continued.

"King Rhadamanthus is much saddened by the loss of his son, but more so by the loss of a new daughter in law." He gestured to me and continued. "The palace has been missing a woman's touch since the loss of our beloved queen several years ago."

There was an awkward silence. I didn't like where

he was going with this.

"As a show of good faith and of the love between our kingdoms and brothers, King Rhadamanthus would like to offer himself as a husband for the fair Ariadne."

His words hit me like a punch to the stomach. Under the table, Phaedre grabbed my hand, which was suddenly freezing. Stunned, I looked to my mother, waiting for her to refute this ridiculous suggestion, but her face never lost its thoughtful expression.

After a beat, my father regained his composure and said, "We are honored that my brother would propose such a union. However, we have decided that Ariadne will not marry. The oracle was quite clear."

Calix turned his gaze to Phaedre, who shrunk back in her chair. She didn't want to be offered up as a consolation prize. King Rhadamanthus was an old man with grown sons and I hadn't even seen him since I was a small child. By marrying me, he would gain control over Knossos and thereby Crete, and after him, his remaining son would retain the throne. The thought of marrying a man almost three times my age, especially one who sired a snake such as Gortys, made me numb and a little dizzy. The contents of my stomach flipped around, threatening to come up. My father couldn't let this happen. I looked from my father to my mother, who sat rigid and still. Why were they not laughing in his face?

"Indeed," Calix responded, "I have heard the prophesy. Burning ships and chaos. Very terrible. King Rhadamanthus believes that this is the solution to such tragedy. A union with him will prevent such an outcome as his love of Crete rivals your own- even more than the love for his child, who died so suddenly and tragically after his visit. Such a death and the loss of a prince causes great sadness, as you well know, Sire. Enough sadness that could lead someone to seek justice."

My father's face hardened. "We are all saddened by Gortys' death. However, it has nothing to do with us. We parted in good faith, and he was far from Knossos when he started to have trouble. It was an unfortunate accident, the work of the gods. There is nothing to seek justice for."

"With the death of a prince, there is always justice to be sought."

Inside, I was screaming, begging for my father to refuse, to defend my happiness, and safeguard my future. Instead, he said. "Very well. I am honored by his proposal and will consider it." With that, I knew it was over.

We finished dinner, but I don't know what was said. I was numb, unable to feel anything except the steady pressure of Phaedre's hand in mine and the suffocating feeling of dread.

* * *

I needed to be alone. After I was released from dinner, I beelined straight for my room, which was now empty. Where had Thalia gone? I paced the floor and then decided that what I needed was air. To my relief, there were no guards outside my door.

As soon as I breathed in the fresh night air and looked up at the blanket of stars, I felt my heart unclench. I walked until I couldn't hear the palace anymore and found myself in a small field, surrounded by the night sky. Flopping down on a large, flat rock, I took a deep breath and listened to the stillness. I wanted to cry or scream. Or both. I tried to cry, but I couldn't. All around me, the squeaks and harmony of nighttime bugs and frogs blended with the silence, and I breathed it in, willing it to soothe me. It didn't.

I picked up a rock, feeling the weight of it in my hand, and hurled it at a nearby tree. It crashed with a satisfying thud and fell to the ground. I picked up another. This time, I threw it harder. Releasing it felt good, cathartic. One after another, I hurled rocks at the tree, releasing the anger that welled up inside of me. I let it course through me. I gave into it. If my mother saw me doing this, she would punish me for sure. This is was not the way a princess behaved, and I didn't care. For the first time maybe ever, I entirely gave into my feelings. I let it out, like a toddler having

162

a fit. So much so that I didn't hear the footsteps coming up behind me.

"Princess. What did that tree do to you?"

When I heard his smooth voice, it startled me. I whipped around to see Dionysus standing behind me with a lopsided grin. My heart leaped into my throat as heat prickled up my face. I wondered how long he'd been watching me.

"Please. Go away. I'm not in the mood," I said, picking up another rock.

"Princess, please. How can I help?" he asked, his amber eyes soft with concern.

"You? I know this is shocking, but not everything is about you." I shot back, regretting it instantly, conscious that I was being too harsh. This wasn't his fault. The problem was that when I looked at him, I didn't see a god. I only saw him, a scruffy, self-confident amber-eyed guy looking at me with concern, and right now, it annoyed me. I was still mad at him for that stunt in the woods, and if I was being honest, for the riot he caused inside me. I looked down at my rocks and found that my supply was dwindling. I picked up a smallish rock and threw it with all my strength. It hit the ground with a pitiful plink.

He smiled. "Well, perhaps a larger rock then." He handed me another, heavier rock, about the size of a quince.

Quince, I thought, fruit sacred to Aphrodite.

Interesting. I hurled it, and it crashed into the ground with a solid crack.

"Yes, that is better. Thanks," I said, still not looking at him.

"What has made you so angry?" he asked, handing me another rock.

"I am to be sold in marriage." Thwack! The rock slammed into the tree.

"Marriage? To who?"

"To my uncle. An old man. With sons older than me." He handed me another rock.

"I see."

"For the love of Crete," I mimicked, scrunching up my face and hurling another rock.

"But, you do love Crete," he said, stooping to pick up a rock.

"Yes. But, he didn't even ask. My father didn't even so much as glance at me."

"Hmm."

"What do you know of this? Your life. You can go where you want. Do what you want. Nobody tells you can't. You're free."

He looked thoughtful. "Yes, I have wandered all over the world, but I can't go everywhere I want." He paused, considering whether to continue. "I know what it is to be in a box because of who you are," he added softly.

I stopped, turned toward him. "What do you mean?"

"The one place I want to go is the one place I'm not allowed."

"Where is that?"

"Olympus. To be at my father's side."

"You're a god. Why can't you go there?"

"I'm a demigod. Only full gods are allowed. My mother was mortal, yes, but not just one of Zeus' conquests. He loved her very much. Enough to swear an oath on the River Styx. An unbreakable oath. His wife has pursued me ever since, hungry for revenge."

I handed him a rock from the growing pile at my feet. He took it with a slow grin and hurled the rock into the forest. I didn't see where it landed.

"It's better if you hit a tree," I said. "You get a better sound that way."

He shook his head. "I have no quarrel with the trees."

I smiled a little, and he tilted his head, looking puzzled.

"It's kind of funny," I said. "You wander all around the world because you can't go home. I'm trapped at home, and all I want to do is see the world. Hera is the goddess of marriage. It seems she has doomed us both."

"Indeed, my princess. Don't worry. You have the spirit of a warrior. Those such as us cannot be kept in cages."

I hoped he was right. For several more minutes, we stood next to each other, throwing rocks and

165

contemplating our cages. I realized that I was feeling better, my spirit felt lighter. When I turned to thank him, he was gone.

~ 11 ~

It was at that point at the end of the slow burn of summer when the sun takes no prisoners.
Energy sapped, we mostly all lounged around the palace trying to keep cool. The only relief came from the strong northern winds, the ones that sometimes lasted for days.

I felt it come, howling through the walls and changing the air. The winds cooled the baked earth, rippled the surface of the sea, and brought another ship. It flew a black sail painted with the royal symbol of Athens and drifted into our main port in the middle of the day. Sails billowing, it glided into the bay, dropped anchor, and waited. It was met by at least thirty of my father's warships, led by the king

167

himself from the deck of our largest ship.

I had visited the port several times, but this was my first time on a ship. Although we were only going out into the harbor, not on a voyage, it was exhilarating. Dressed in my finest clothes and jewelry, I stood at the helm with my family, my hands resting on the solid wood of the ship, and imagined I was going on a grand adventure. The ship bobbed in the choppy water.

The best ships in the fleet waited in formation, with my family perched on the deck of the largest one, accompanied by 100 of our best soldiers. Although he didn't wear his battle armor, my father's sword hung at his belt and he looked every inch a great king. Beside him, my mother sparkled with jewels and held her head high, a united front surrounded by the strength of Crete. The ship rocked and swayed, moving with the choppy water. My hair whipped in the wind. My father gave the signal and the soldiers on the oars nudged us forward.

As we glided closer to the other ship, a gust of wind blew through, and then everything went still. Water lapped the side of the ship and nobody moved. We knew who was on the ship. Rumors circled about Theseus' grand arrival in Athens and his subsequent departure. This was the year of the tribute and we'd heard Theseus volunteered himself. We didn't know what else waited on his ship. My father would never show apprehension, but it showed in the stiffness of his stance and the forced calm on his face.

I looked around at our fleet and felt pride. Theseus was a warrior, but this time, he wasn't up against an old woman with a sow or a crazy old man with a deadly bed. We had the most powerful navy in the land and it would take more than a bronze club to best us. Phaedre pressed against me and we craned our necks trying to get a look at him.

We soon realized that Theseus wasn't accompanied by soldiers. He wasn't even wearing armor. He was surrounded by children. We brought an army to meet a single warrior and a group of children.

Our ship slid in close and my father called out. "Theseus, honored son of King Aegeus. I bid you welcome."

Theseus walked to the helm, directly ahead of us. Next to me, Phaedre caught her breath. Even in a simple tunic, Theseus radiated power and confidence and looked like the hero he was rumored to be, tall with broad shoulders and dark cropped hair. Unconcerned with the army before him, Theseus beamed at my father, appearing genuinely happy to be arriving at our shores. As I looked around, gods help me, I felt a little foolish. Our ship filled with warriors looked not like a display of strength, but one of power.

"King Minos. I bring you the last tribute from Athens." His voice was clear and deep, emphasizing the word "last."

My father raised his eyebrow in amusement. "The last?"

"Yes," Theseus replied. "This is the last tribute you will get from Athens."

"You should not have come," my father responded. "In doing so, you deprive your father of his only heir."

Theseus laughed. "Have no fear, my lord. I will easily slay your Minotaur and return safely to my father, along with the tribute." The children behind him were still, like little statues.

A bolt of lightning ripped across the sky.

"The God of the Sky is threatening you." My father said, gesturing to the sky, a sure sign that Zeus was displeased.

Theseus threw his arms wide, basking in the sky. "No. He is welcoming me."

My father chuckled. "We shall see. Care to prove it?"

Theseus seemed to consider for a moment and then nodded his agreement. My father took off his royal ring and held it up. "Will the God of the Sea also welcome you?" With a flourish, he tossed it into the ocean. My mother gasped and grabbed his arm. "Let Poseidon help you return my ring." My father looked smug. He never doubted for a moment whose side the gods were on.

Without responding, Theseus dove into the water, making a ripple rather than a splash. For several moments, our whole ship collectively held its breath. We waited. No bubbles broke the surface. I shifted from foot to foot, watching for him to emerge. Phaedre leaned forward, expectant.

Minutes later, a dolphin leaped out of the water in a graceful arch. Like an otter, Theseus' head popped up, dark and slick. He swam over to our ship, and after one of the soldiers released the rope ladder, he bounded up. In one swift motion, he swung over onto the deck, dripping wet. He moved like water, loose and flowing. Sauntering past the soldiers, he was unconcerned about his dripping wet tunic, clinging to every muscle. Phaedre, my mother and I all tried not to notice. Theseus was my enemy, sent here by the king who had my brother killed. I was trying so hard not to look at his square jaw and muscled chest that at first, I didn't even see what he held. In his hand, he had not only the ring but also a golden crown, sparkling with seven points with seven jewels. A family of dolphins splashed and played in the water behind him.

He bowed deeply and moved to approach our family. The soldiers pitched forward to intercept him, but my father raised his hand and they fell back. Still dripping wet, Theseus moved forward, pausing in front of Phaedre. She glittered beneath his gaze and flashed him a smile, clearly pleased to have his attention. Inexplicably, he turned from her to me and held out the crown. "Princess," he said, bowing his

171

head, "Such a treasure deserves a beauty such as yours."

Stunned, I looked to my father for guidance on how to respond. He nodded and I lowered my head. Theseus gently placed the crown on my head. Despite the heavy jewels, it felt light, like it was made for me. In it, I felt beautiful, which was a curious feeling. When I raised my head, I looked up into his striking blue eyes, which were intently studying my face. I felt his eyes slide over the rest of my body. My cheeks flushed and I shifted uncomfortably on my feet, but I didn't look away. For a moment, I couldn't breathe. His eyes held mine and lightning shot through my body down to the bottom of my feet.

With a slight smile, Theseus turned to my father, holding out the ring.

"Your ring, Sire," he said, bowing his head.

"Impressive," my father said. Then, turning to address the soldiers, he added.

"Poseidon honors us today. Not only did he recover my ring, but he sent my daughter, Ariadne, a beautiful crown as a gift. Once again, the gods smile on Crete!" As the soldiers cheered, Phaedre stiffened beside me. The warrior had arrived.

~ 12 ~

The next day was a blur. Theseus and the children were given rooms of honor to await the ceremony. They weren't prisoners, but they also weren't allowed to leave. Stories about Theseus and his arrival swirled, growing with each telling. Talk and decisions surrounding my possible marriage faded into the background, which was just fine with me. Calix, however, had taken to sulking around the palace, but I'm not sure anyone besides me noticed. With Theseus' grand entrance, excitement for the tribute exploded and everyone's attention turned to preparing for it.

The only one who wasn't getting a feast was Asterion. He needed to be kept hungry. Since Theseus' arrival, I wasn't allowed into the labyrinth to feed him, which made me sad. I imagined him coming out at the usual time, looking for his basket, only to find the little table empty. He was a monster, but I hoped he wouldn't think I deserted him. I was all he had.

My mother took to her room and didn't come out. In her absence, Phaedre happily assumed the duty of overseeing the preparations. For years, she was the apprentice and now, she relished the leading role, sashaying about ordering the servants and everyone, including me, around. After a morning of Phaedre following me around with her list of things to do, I escaped to check on my mother. I found her pacing in her room. Even agitated and slightly disheveled, she seemed to float back and forth across the floor.

"Stupid girl. She couldn't even kill him when he was right in front of her." There was nobody else in the room. Unsure if she knew I was there, I stepped into the light so she could see me.

"Who mother?" I said.

She didn't acknowledge me. "Any idiot can hide poison. Now, I'm left with her mess."

After a moment of confusion, I realized she was talking about Medea, Theseus' stepmother, who tried to poison him when he arrived in Athens. It was a favorite story around the palace.

It was shocking to see my mother like this. My normally composed mother, the Queen, was pacing and ranting like a fisherman's wife.

"And now he's here. What does he want? Isn't it enough they took my Androgeos? Now, they want Crete too. This is our right. What they owe us." She still hadn't noticed me.

"Because of their treachery," I offered, trying to get her attention.

She glanced at me and kept on as if I hadn't spoken. Her voice hardened. "It's all I have left of my son. His memory and their blood."

After a while, I convinced her to lie down and I went out looking for chamomile for tea to calm her nerves. There was none in her herb chest. So, I left her with her attendants and advised them to watch over her and not let her leave. It wouldn't be suitable for anyone else to see her in that state. Although, if she wanted to leave, I'm not sure anyone could stop her.

Truthfully, I was eager to get outside into the fresh air. It was pretty thick in the palace and after everything that happened, I needed a break. I also needed to find Thalia. I felt like I'd barely seen her in weeks and I missed her. We had much to talk about and my head swam. I needed to ground myself in her, to talk through everything and sort through my feelings. Also, there was Darius. Now that he was allowed to marry, everything would change for her. I wanted her to know I was happy and excited for her, that at least one of us would have the future we desired. I set out looking for Thalia first, but my thoughts kept coming back to Androgeos.

175

He had been gone since I was a small child, but his presence was everywhere. He was in the faraway look my mother sometimes got as she sat at her loom and in my father's heavy steps. He was in the silence around the corners in the palace, that thing that was missing. When I crossed the fields, I almost expected him to fly past on his horse. I remember when he left for the games in Athens, confident and sure, the pride of our island. Of course he did well. How could he not? He was made for the games. When he didn't come home, rumors spread. Some said that he was robbed and killed on the way home. Others said it was no accident, that King Aegeus sent men to kill him. I was just a child. Nobody told me anything and I didn't understand. I waited for him to return. Every day, I watched the port for his ship to dock, willing it to appear on the horizon. I made him toys and sculptures made of rocks and sticks, longing for him to sweep me up in his arms and call me his little monkey.

Instead, his body arrived in a ship flying black sails. My mother's scream ripped through the sky up to Zeus himself. I held Alcina's hand during the funeral procession and walked behind my parents. Phaedre was just a baby and was carried by her nursemaid. Up ahead, the musicians told his story in song and the sweet notes from the flute pulled us forward. Usually, after the procession moves through a village, people go back to their homes. For Androgeos, the people

176

followed. By the time we reached the burial site, the procession had stretched back further than I could see. His people loved him. I loved him. I buried my face in Alcina's robes when he was carried into the burial chamber.

When we razed Athens to the ground, it was Alcina who gave me the news, but only after I stumbled upon her crying. I remember the ships returning victorious to cheering crowds and feasting that lasted for days. Later, when the tribute came, I wasn't allowed out. Phaedre and I were kept in our rooms, where Alcina fussed over us with pursed lips.

I missed my brother every day. Aside from Thalia, he was the only one who saw me and loved me anyway. I missed his quick smile and gentle nature, but also what he was. If he were here, he would ensure the safety of Crete. He would be the heir. Now, that weight rested on me. The oracle would never proclaim destruction when she read his future. My uncle would stay on his own shore and I could marry who I pleased. Well, maybe not exactly who I wished, but my husband would seek me, not a kingdom. Athens took all of that away. In his place, there was a hole that nobody could fill. For this loss, Athens owes us this tribute. It stopped the wars and brought peace, just like my brother would have done had he lived.

I found Thalia in the stores, getting more supplies for the cooks. As soon as I saw her, the heaviness from thinking of Androgeos disappeared. It didn't take much to convince her to accompany me and we walked together to drop off a barrel of flour before heading outside in search of chamomile for my mother. The sky was a glorious blue broken only by a single cloud. Early autumn flowers brightened the fields, sweetening the air with their light scent. I breathed in deeply, relieved for a snippet of freedom and happy to be with Thalia.

In a rush, I told her of Theseus and the ring and the crown, although I knew she already knew. I gushed on. I told her of his deep blue eyes and the way he walked and how the crown made me feel. I wanted to gossip with her about how his legs looked in his short tunic and what it meant that he gave the crown to me and not Phaedre, but she was curiously silent. We combed the hillside for almost an hour with me chattering on until I started to get frustrated at our one-sided conversation.

"Thalia," I started, stopping to face her. "My world has turned upside down and you don't seem to care. I've barely seen you lately and when I do, you're far away. Where have you been?"

"Where have I been? Are you serious?" she snapped.

"Yes. Is Darius really so much more important-"

"Darius?" she interrupted. "Is that what you think this is about?"

"What what is about? I don't understand..."

"No, you wouldn't."

"What do you mean?"

"Your life is upside down? Because you might have to marry a prince. You're still here, surrounded by servants. You weave. You live your life. You go to sleep and don't worry about being roused from your bed."

I flinched like I'd been hit. Her tone was hard and brisk and she was looking at me expecting an answer, but I didn't know what to say. I was confused. I really had no idea why she was so angry. "What are you talking about?" I asked.

"Where do you think I've been every night?" she asked.

"I don't know. I thought you were with Darius."

"Darius! No. How can I see him like this? His heart would break. No, I haven't been with Darius."

"Then where?"

"Are you that blind? Your father has been summoning me."

"My father?"

"Did you not know that happened? That your precious father, who you think is so kind and just, summons the servant girls to his bed? Apparently, I am of the right age now."

My chest tightened, my breath caught in my throat. I was shocked. I tried to picture my dignified father, so in love with my mother, doing such a thing. I didn't know what to say. "My father?" I repeated, dumb.

"He is a man like any other."

"No. He is the King."

"Exactly."

My mind raced as I tried to make sense of this. I stared at her, not knowing what to do or how to fix it, not knowing how to return to normal. But then, the pieces started to fit together. Him whispering with her during the banquet for the suitors. How she disappeared every night. How the other servants moved out of her way when she passed by. Her sadness.

"Oh Thalia," I said, moving toward her to embrace her.

"Don't," she said, holding up her hand. "Just don't."

She grabbed the basket of chamomile and beelined back to the palace. I stood helpless, watching her disappear and not wanting to move. Not wanting to go back to the palace. Not wanting to do anything. Wanting what she said to not be true. I thought of her and Darius holding hands on the way to the market, and how he always glanced at her when she wasn't looking.

How had I not noticed this happening right in front of me? I was so wrapped up in my own drama. My god, I was annoyed that she wasn't there. I didn't even think about why she wasn't. I thought she was acting selfish, choosing Darius over me, but it was me. I failed her. I should have known. However, even now that I did know, there was nothing I could do to stop it. He was my father, the King. The highest power aside from the gods. Then, a thought stopped me cold. My mother. What would she do when she found out?

I did the only thing that made sense. I ran. Until my lungs burned more than the pain in my chest. Over rocks and up dirt paths until I could see the water and smell the salt. I ran to the cliffs, where the waves crashed into the rocks. I stood next to the edge, breathing fast and hard, trying to catch my breath and let the rhythm of the waves drown out Thalia's voice in my head. How had I not known what was right in front of me? I kept seeing her face, filled with anger and hurt. It was my fault. I should have known.

A rustling in the brush startled me out of my head. I looked around to see someone coming toward me. Of course, Theseus didn't feel the need to be quiet. He stomped over flowers, making enough noise for a whole army. When he saw me he stopped abruptly.

"Princess," he said with an exaggerated bow.

"Prince." I nodded in return. "Are you so eager to see the sea after your voyage? Or are you running away?"

He tilted his head and offered a bemused smile. "No, lady. I don't run away."

"Then, what brings you out here?"

"I wanted to see something beautiful."

"I love the sea," I replied, looking out over the

turquoise waves, softening a bit.

"I was not speaking of the sea." I felt his eyes on me and my face flushed.

"Why are you in Crete?" I asked.

"For peace. I already told you. I will slay your Minotaur and end this terror."

"Indeed?"

He raised an eyebrow and grinned at me, confident in his ability to charm me. I looked at his smug face and I had the overwhelming urge to punch him.

"He has defeated better men than you. Besides, I thought you Athenians liked to send thieves to do your dirty work."

A brief flicker of confusion rolled across his face before his striking blue eyes settled on a thoughtful expression.

He sighed. "You have spirit. I'll give you that. I didn't know your brother and I am truly sorry he is not here. His kindness and bravery are spoken of everywhere."

I half expected him to deny it, to tell me the well-worn story that my brother was set upon by thieves or that he somehow deserved to die. His kind words startled me as much as his overconfidence unnerved me.

"He was." I didn't know what to say to this stranger. I stopped and looked back out over the waves, letting their rhythm calm my pounding heart. I replied softly, "He didn't deserve what you did to him."

"Lady, I didn't do anything to him. It was a tragedy, but he has been avenged. Your father's navy destroyed entire towns. Athens has paid for what happened to him."

"That's not for you to decide."

"Athens decided. Our villages were razed, our children taken, and sent to atone for a crime they didn't commit. The people are angry. If I am to win them, we must have peace." He gestured to the palace. "Those children weren't even alive when your brother was killed. You have to see that." He looked so earnest. I almost believed he was on a mission of peace.

Nobody had ever talked to me like this before, like it mattered what I thought, and I searched for the right words to respond. I didn't feel like arguing with him, but Crete wasn't the villain here. The tribute was our due from an injustice done to us, payment for their treachery. If their people were unhappy, it was their own fault.

"It is the price of peace," I said.

"And Athens has paid it."

"Why do you even care? From what I hear, you only just arrived in Athens and your welcome was not very happy."

"Athens is my home. It's my birthright. The witch Medea could not keep me away. Neither will your monster."

183

"That remains to be seen."

"I don't wish for war with Crete," he said after a long pause.

"No?"

He smiled and placed a hand on my shoulder. "If I wanted that, what would stop me from pushing you off this cliff?" He said it playfully, but what he said was true. There was nobody here. If he decided to harm me, there was nothing I could do. I took a few steps away from the edge. He chuckled.

"No, no, Princess. Don't be afraid. I have no wish to harm you. I merely meant that if I wanted vengeance on Crete, there are other ways to achieve it. I could have arrived with a ship of warriors instead of a ship of scared children."

I couldn't argue with that. He arrived in Crete like an honored guest, not a warrior.

"I must get back." I needed to get away from him, from his broad shoulders and his lazy smile that started in his eyes and ended in a dimple in his left cheek. From the way he looked at my face when he talked and listened for a response. In a rush, I brushed past him and left him on the cliff. I didn't look back, but I could feel his gaze follow me down the path.

~ 13 ~

I spent most of the next morning spinning thread while my mother worked at her loom. Phaedre was busy overseeing preparations for the upcoming banquet, so it was just my mother and me in the weaving room. All traces of the state I found her in after Theseus arrived were gone. If anything, she looked even more radiant. With her blond hair smooth and tied back with a jeweled barrette and her robes almost translucent against her pale skin, she could have been the Goddess herself. If she was still feeling anxious about Theseus, she didn't show it. Her mask never slipped. I tried to broach the subject a few times, but she wouldn't bite. When we did talk, it was of the weather and the banquet and most definitely not about the warrior sleeping in the men's wing, Thalia, or whether they were going to marry me off to my uncle.

The unspoken words were a third person in the room with us, making the hole in the conversation grow by the minute. I was getting restless and when I asked permission to visit my brother's tomb to place an offering, she readily agreed, as long as I bring a guard with me. I bolted from the weaving room and ran off to gather my things. Before leaving, I looked around for Thalia, but she was nowhere to be found.

I hoped she was just working and not attending to my father. I shuddered to think of her with him and I hoped she was all right. Guilt picked at me, but I didn't want to wait for her. I didn't really feel like talking to anybody. I headed toward the tomb, first checking to make sure Calix wasn't around. Ever since that dinner where my future was casually tossed around, I successfully avoided crossing paths with him. I didn't want to think about him or the questions he brought from my uncle.

Outside the palace, the bright autumn sunshine recharged me, warmed my face and relaxed my body. My feet felt light. With the guard trailing behind me, I picked up my pace, stopping to collect flowers along the way. For a brief moment, I considered bringing some for Asterion before I realized I couldn't.

I followed the winding road toward my brother's burial chamber and the closer I got, the calmer I felt.

His burial chamber, dug into a hill and sealed, would be the final resting place of my family and it should have made me feel sad. It didn't. Coming here always filled me with a sense of peace and grounding, like I belonged to something. For me, this was not a place of sadness. If anything, it was the one place where it didn't seem like my brother was missing. When the colorful door of the chamber came into view, I was surprised to see someone else kneeling at the altar.

Seeing Calix, my stomach clenched. He was the last person I wanted to talk to, but it was too late to turn around. He already saw me.

"Princess," he said, raising a hand to greet me. A broad smile spread over his face as he stood up to bow.

"Calix," I responded without enthusiasm. "What are you doing here?" He looked surprised by the ice in my voice.

"Just paying respects to an old friend."

Now, I was surprised. "You knew my brother?"

"Of course. When I was a boy, my father sent me here to learn archery. Your brother had the best teachers. So, I spent some time here, but you were quite small. You probably don't remember."

I searched my memories for a boy, tall and lanky with Calix's angular features, but there was nothing.

"No, I'm sorry. I don't remember."

"Well, as I said, you were quite small. I do remember you though, always chasing behind us.

187

Your nurse... what was her name?"

"Alcina."

"Yes, Alcina. She was always running after you, trying to get you to act like a princess." He chuckled.

In spite of myself, I smiled at the memory.

"His loss was... tremendous. I still think of him often. I brought him this," he said, showing me a small, delicate bronze orchid.

"It's beautiful."

"Yes. Androgeos had it made for me to give to Lyssa before we were married. She was so beautiful and I was such a fool for her. I couldn't even speak around her." He chuckled. "All my words disappeared. He told me to tell her it reminded me of her beauty, or some such thing. He had a whole speech for me to say."

I smiled again, remembering my suave brother. "Did it work?"

He laughed. "Not really. My Lyssa is not like the other girls who came to court." He studied me for a moment. "I suspect she is more like you, not impressed by shiny things and empty words."

"So, what happened?"

"I couldn't remember what I was supposed to say. I could barely look at her. She liked the flower though and she kept talking to me. She always kept it as a memory of our first meeting, but when I see it, I remember your brother. I thought it fitting to return it to him."

"Well, I'm sure he was glad that you found happiness." Despite my best efforts, I was enjoying Calix's company.

"You will find happiness as well," he said. I nodded in response.

"I also brought offerings. Do you want to join me?" I asked.

"No, thank you. I don't want to intrude. I should be getting back to the palace. Your father wanted to speak with me."

"Of course," I said, feeling oddly sorry to see him go, this person who knew my brother. I wanted to hear all of his stories about Androgeos. Also, the less time Calix spent talking to my father, the better.

"You know. He's not as bad as you think."

"Who?"

"King Rhadamanthus. He's older, it's true. But, he's kind. He's not Gortys. He won't be unfair to you. You will be safe there. Perhaps you will meet my Lyssa. You two would get along well."

I nodded. Why was everyone always interested in keeping me safe? "I hope to meet her someday. Under different circumstances."

"Ahh. I understand. If your father agrees to the match, you don't need to worry. You will have friends in Phaistos."

With a brief nod, he turned and started down the pathway. He looked back and waved. As he walked away, I realized I was unfair to him. He was only

189

doing what he was asked by his king. It was comforting to know I would have a friend in an unfamiliar court if it came to that. However, the thought of marrying his king turned my stomach. He was almost as old as my father. No matter how kind he was, with him, I wouldn't be a partner as my parents were partners. I would be locked away, bred and brought out as a showpiece. I was his key to power and nothing else. I shuddered as I thought of having to endure his old hands on me. Guilt slipped into me. I had an overwhelming urge to go find Thalia and beg her forgiveness. I refused to believe that was our destiny.

Was it foolish to hope for more than a union of power? To think I could have love? I had to have been made for more than just a path to a throne.

I shook my head to jar myself out of these thoughts. Slowly, my attention returned to my brother and the task at hand. I retrieved my offering from my bag and laid it out on the altar. It was a hand-carved horse that he'd given me when I was a child. That's how I liked to remember him, flying past me on the back of his horse, laughing wildly with his long hair streaming behind him. I removed a swatch of the light airy fabric that usually floated around my mother and wove it around his marker, making it look like a statue in a cloud. My fingers trailed over the cool marble of his face carved into the stone, beautiful but formal. It was expertly crafted and a good likeness, but the eyes were blank. They lacked his spark.

Before I left, I pulled out a little satchel of dried thyme. When someone dies, we burn thyme during the funeral rites to lend strength for his journey and guide him to the afterlife. It wasn't necessary to do it again, but I wanted his tomb to be cleansed and it was all I could do for him. As I lit it, the fragrant smoke wrapped around me. I breathed deeply, filling my lungs, wanting it to fortify me with the strength of the thyme and the strength of my brother.

When the little pile had burned to ash, I was ready for the banquet and ready for what comes ahead. My brother was with me. Together, we headed back to the palace.

It had never been suggested before that I wear anything of my mother's, much less her sheer pale dress, the one that made her look like she was wrapped in moonlight. I didn't hold the illusion that I resembled her, but with the light fabric skimming my body, I felt graceful. I stood taller, held my head up straight. My hair hung loose down my back, held in place by a bronze clasp. The only jewelry I wore was a bronze bracelet that wound up my arm. My mother didn't press when I didn't want to wear the kohl to darken my eyes, but she did insist I wear the crown to show our appreciation for Poseidon who gave it to me, even though we both knew it wasn't Poseidon who gave it to me. It was Theseus.

We gathered in the main courtyard, which was

filled with my father's associates, nobles and courtiers. Oil lamps threw golden light, making the walls flicker and glow. Our festivals always start with a dance. Since this one celebrates the harvest, our dance is a celebration of the Goddess. Since I was the oldest, my dance started the night. I loved dancing. The notes from the lyre floated around me, urging me to begin. I started slowly, stretching my arms and feeling the music move through my body. The melody was slow and winding and I moved in time with it. I closed my eyes, letting the music guide me, feeling the fabric of my dress brush my hips as they swayed.

I twirled, my scarf floating behind me as I snaked through the circular labyrinth pattern. All of the children sat together, the ones from Athens and the ones from Crete. I passed my scarf over them and smiled into Theseus' intense face. The directness of his look startled me, but I didn't shrink away from it. I glanced over my shoulder as I swept away from him, enjoying the way it felt to be watched by him, feeling his gaze follow me. As the force of the music flowed through me, even he disappeared. I lost myself. The room faded away and I just danced.

The last note hung in the air for a moment before the musicians picked up the tempo. Out of breath, I bowed to my parents and moved to the side as more people joined the dance floor. Dancing was the one thing I did that seemed to make my mother happy

192

and she looked on me now with pride. I stood, a little breathless and feeling beautiful in my mother's blue dress as the other dancers started to swirl. They formed a semi-circle, linked by touching each other's wrists, while their feet moved in sync to the music. The song picked up in a joyful melody.

In the middle, Phaedre glided, graceful and radiant, anchoring the dance. On either side of her, two of my father's high ranking soldiers jostled for her attention. She smiled at them, but she wasn't looking at the soldiers. Her eyes slid past them over to the side, to where Theseus stood. They stayed there, willing him to look at her, but he didn't. Instead, he watched the children giggle and bounce to the music.

A light breeze brushed my face. I looked again at the children on the floor, all bathed and dressed in loose cotton clothing. They were up now, forming their own circle. Giggling and hesitant, the younger ones mimicking the movements they saw on the circular stage and the older ones a little more confident, showing them the way. A few of the older girls were only a bit younger than me and already were graceful and practiced in their movements. They all blended together, making it difficult to see which were from Athens and which from Crete. They were all just children. As I watched them having fun together, I wondered if they knew what lay ahead. The thought made me turn away and suddenly, the courtyard felt too crowded. I needed some space.

Needing to see the stars, I made my way over to the side, where the pathway led outside, enjoying the gentle breeze it allowed through the courtyard. Thankfully, it was empty. I didn't feel like making idle conversation. I stood in the doorway, looking out over the darkness where stars scattered like sand across the sky.

"Your dance..."

Startled, I spun around to see Theseus leaning against a wall. I didn't even hear him walk up.

"How long have you been standing there?"

He grinned, amused to see me off balance. "Not long."

I glanced toward the dancers. All eyes followed Phaedre, which was right where she wanted them to be.

"You're the guest of honor. You're missing Phaedre's dance."

He shrugged. "I saw the dance I wanted to see."

I colored and looked away. "I just needed some air."

"Me too."

"The crown," he said. "It suits you. Like it was made for you."

I nodded my thanks. I burned to ask him why he gave it to me instead of Phaedre, but I let the moment pass.

Silence stretched between us, broken only by the music floating out from the courtyard.

"Is it true that Medea tried to poison you?" I said.

"She tried. She's long gone now."

"My mother says she is a foolish witch."

"A witch yes. Foolish no. It is a mistake to underestimate her."

I've always been fascinated by my cousin, Medea, probably because my mother won't talk about her. To me, Medea was wild and dangerous, always walking the edge between self-interest and self destruction. To my mother, she was an embarrassment. I wanted to ask him about her, but the look on his face told me the subject was closed.

"Your father truly didn't know you?"

"I was raised by my mother. He never saw me." He looked down.

I imagined Theseus making his way across the land, searching for his father, doing deeds of bravery to make his father proud only to finally make it to his doorstep and not be recognized. It seemed like a lonely path.

"How did he finally recognize you?" I asked.

"My sword. I drew my sword at his treacherous wife. It was the one he left under the rock when he left. He saw it and recognized it."

"And then you left him to come here."

"I had no choice. Athens was in an uproar. This tribute of yours-"

"Not mine."

"The people don't support it. They are tired of giving their sons and daughters to Crete, while the nobility keeps theirs. They were gathering weapons. I volunteered because my father needed me."

"It will crush him when you don't return. He has not even gotten to know you properly."

He smiled. "Lady, I will return to him."

"Hmm," I said. "How do you plan to do that?"

"I already told you. I will kill the Minotaur."

"Hmm."

"Why do you doubt me? I already killed its father. I will finish the job."

Although I longed to hear how he killed the famous white bull, I didn't ask. We were not friends and I couldn't let him think I was some foolish girl, hanging on to his tales of bravery. Instead, I said nothing. He studied me with a casual intensity that unnerved me.

"We should get back," I said, indicating the banquet. "Your disappearance will be noticed."

"Then, let us go," he said, holding out his arm.

After a pause, I took it and we started back inside.

"Well, here you are!" Phaedre bounded up to us, all cheer and smiles, looking from me to him, then to my hand on his arm. I quickly dropped my hand. She shifted, putting her back to me and shining her brilliant smile on Theseus. "Father is so pleased you are here. He called it a gesture of goodwill that King Aegeus should lose his son the way we lost ours."

He bowed his head, but didn't respond. "Come," she said, inserting herself between us and latching on to his arm. "You must join the dancing." She beamed up at him, a coy smile spreading over her face. "Perhaps we can partner for the Sousta."

I was shocked at her boldness. The Sousta was a dance of war and seduction. It's a partner dance, but usually done by married or established couples due to the complexity and the level of coordination involved. Traditionally, the King and Queen led this dance and it was the perfect showcase of my mother's beauty and skill. When my parents dance, there might as well be nobody else in the room. It would be highly inappropriate for a maiden princess to dance this with anyone, let alone a stranger.

Theseus removed himself from her grasp. "Umm. I regret that I'm not much of a dancer. I would hate to misstep and embarrass such a gracious partner." Then, turning to me, he added "Perhaps, Ariadne can explain it to me since this is not a dance we do in Athens." Phaedre's expression turned hard like a beautiful, marble statue.

"Perhaps," she said, turning on her heels and heading back to the crowd. Theseus held out his arm to me again.

"Ready?"

Back inside, the music was faster, the wine was flowing and the mood was warm. A circle of children and adults joined hands and moved in and out to the music, like a giggling heartbeat. We watched for a moment before Phaedre pounced again. I stayed off to the side, smiling as she pulled Theseus reluctantly into the circle. It was only a matter of time, really. He who had fought thieves and monsters couldn't extricate himself from Phaedre's grasp. What she wants, she usually gets. I chuckled, thinking he had met his match.

Watching him fumbling as he tried to keep up made me giggle and when he caught me watching, he bit his lip and gave me a playful grimace. He and Phaedre were so natural together, even though he made a show of resisting it. As I watched them dance, I found my thoughts turning to Dionysus, wondering if he had learned our dances. I looked around, hoping to see a stray grapevine or flower, but the walls were bare. I stood by myself, silently watching the dancers fold in around each other.

~ 14 ~

When I knew I wouldn't be missed, I slipped out of the banquet and went in search of Thalia. I didn't find her in any of the places I expected. With a sinking feeling, I realized that she might be in my father's quarters. The thought of finding her there made me feel sick, but I had this overwhelming urge to find her. We needed to settle things. Following the winding corridors, I kept my footsteps soft, careful not to be heard as I made my way through the men's wing.

A giggle, soft and light, floated just ahead, followed by the deep murmur of voices. I stopped. Was it Thalia? I stilled my breathing and listened. No, not Thalia. Her laugh was throatier, more contagious. No, that was Phaedre's giggle. Not knowing what to do, I pressed myself against the wall, fitting into the shadow thrown by the torch. What was she doing out in the men's quarters and who was she with? More muffled talking and Phaedre's breathy laughter. I strained to hear.

"You're just saying that…", Phaedre said.

"…. Most beautiful…"

Phaedre's voice, flirty and playful. "You are going to get me in trouble."

"Trouble? No. I'm going to make you a queen."

Theseus. His voice rumbled thick and low. I leaned in closer, but I couldn't hear anything more. My face flushed hot at the rustle of clothing and the stifled voices. Curiosity turned to panic as I turned and darted back the way I came.

Still reeling from what I'd heard, I wanted to find Thalia more than ever. The palace corridors wound and curved back on themselves, and I slipped down another hall that led to my father's room. I turned a corner to see two guards on either side of his door. I paused for a moment, thinking of how to explain my presence here and my need to get into my father's room. Nothing believable sprang to mind. Even if I came out and asked them, they wouldn't tell me if Thalia was in there and they would tell my father that I was where I shouldn't be. I sat for a moment, with my back pressed against the wall, thinking of what to do. Short of overpowering the guards and forcing my way in, I couldn't think of any way to get into my father's room. This was a dead end. Even if she was inside, there there was nothing I could do about it. I turned around and went back to my room. Hopefully, I could find her tomorrow. I missed her and I really needed to make things right with her.

Later, I tossed and turned and chased sleep, but I couldn't get my mind to stop talking. My thoughts raced over my dance and how Theseus' eyes felt on me. Had I imagined that? I didn't think so. Remembering the quiet of the night air and how Phaedre's face looked when she stormed away made me feel anxious. I thought we were getting closer, but she was so angry. Why? She knew my fate was to remain here unmarried. Judging by the scene in the hallway, she seemed to get what she wanted anyway. He knew exactly which button to push with her. Queen. It's all she had ever wanted. Nevermind that his presence here was a threat to Crete. I wasn't sure what she was playing at, but it made me nervous.

Intermingled with those thoughts, I kept seeing the children from Athens dancing and laughing with the ones from Crete. They were just children. I wondered who was missing them at home and whether they were sleeping. Thalia's pallet beside me remained empty and I had nobody to talk to. My thoughts chased each other over and over until I thought I would go mad.

I willed myself to stop thinking. Unable to stand it

anymore, I got up and paced around the room. I stretched and took some deep breaths. When I laid back down, my eyes wouldn't stay shut. I'd squeeze them shut and they'd pop back open in an endless cycle. Finally, I couldn't lay there anymore. I looked over at Thalia's untouched bed, stood up, got dressed and grabbed my shawl. I didn't bother to contain my hair.

There was one guard outside my door and he was sound asleep. I stepped over his legs and padded through the quiet palace. I pulled my shawl tighter around me and stepped into the cool, night air. The stars overhead spread out forever. I followed them away from the palace through the plain toward the olive grove. Around me, crickets chirped while a breeze rustled the branches. I closed my eyes, took a deep breath, savoring the green and woody smell from the olive trees.

In the clearing, I saw torches and heard the drum beats. Like I was on fishing line, the commotion pulled me forward. As I got closer, I saw the women twirling with their fawn skin dresses and pine cone wands. I watched them for a moment, and then noticed someone sitting by himself on the side of the hill.

With his arms wrapped around his knees and his head resting on his arms, Dionysus lost lost. I sat down next to him. Silence unrolled between us.

"What makes the God of Wine miss the party?" I

asked, trying to break the silence. He looked over, gave me a shadow of his lopsided grin.

"What makes a princess wander around the darkness by herself?"

"I asked you first."

He chuckled. "I don't feel much like the God of Wine tonight."

"Why not?"

He paused a moment, as if thinking of how to respond. "The thing about wine is that it makes you more of what you are. It's truth. Sometimes the truth is freedom and sometimes, not. Tonight, it feels heavy."

"Why?"

"You ask a lot of questions." He smiled.

"So I've been told."

He swept his hand toward his followers down the hill from us. "They have freedom. Each other. Sometimes, I wonder how I got here. It was easier when I was just Dio, the kid climbing around the mountains. The one who didn't have to have the answers. Does that make sense?"

It did. I thought of how it felt waiting to start my race with the other girls or lately, how it felt to tag along with Thalia and Darius. Separate. Apart. I leaned over and bumped against his shoulder with mine. "It does."

After a while, I asked if he wanted to join them.

"No. Just sit with me. Being near you helps."

203

The drum beats floated up the hill as his followers continued their revelry. We sat, shoulder to shoulder under the stars watching them spin and laugh. The heaviness lifted.

* * *

It was late when I came back to my rooms. When I woke up, I felt like I hadn't slept at all and the last place I wanted to go was to the weaving room. I dragged myself out of bed. After the hallway last night, I didn't want to see Phaedre and I didn't know what to say to her when I did. However, when my mother's attendant came and summoned me, I went. It wasn't much of a choice. At least it was something familiar that I could concentrate on.

Since finishing the tapestry, we had moved on to a more delicate weave, the kind which produced the airy, flowing robes my mother favored. The fabric we worked on today was golden, almost the color of Phaedre's hair. With my mother's fair coloring, she preferred cooler colors, silvers and blues, so this fabric was not for her. Since my future was uncertain, it was not for me. The color and the way the fabric shimmered would make my beautiful sister look like a sun goddess. I wondered if this meant Phaedre would soon be coming out for a husband. I looked over at her standing at the loom. Phaedre's face looked drawn, like she'd been up all night. She didn't acknowledge me, so I didn't say anything and took my place with the distaff and spindle to wind the thread.

It was just the two of us and despite the silence that hung in the air, we soon set into a rhythm. Normally, without the stern eye of our mother, we would sing our favorite love songs or tell stories or gossip. Today, it was just the thunk thunk thunk of Phaedre banging each new row up to the top of the loom. After a while, the silence became overpowering.

"Phaedre," I said, wanting to ask her about Theseus. Did he hurt her? Is that why she was acting so odd? "Are you all right?"

She jerked up from her weaving, her face bright. "Of course. Why wouldn't I be?"

"I don't know. You just seem quiet."

"I'm fine." She said it through clenched teeth, paused a moment and then huffed, "I'm not the one who was making a fool of myself in that ridiculous crown."

"Oh," I said, realization dawning. "That crown. Is that what this is about? Theseus? I have no inter-"

"Oh please. As If I would want an Athenian traitor who will be dead by nightfall." Her words had venom, but she said them a little too quickly with too much effort to sound flippant. I remembered his voice from the hallway. *I will make you a queen.*

"He might succeed, you know," I offered, trying to draw her out. "He has slain other beasts."

205

"Not like ours."

That was true. Our Minotaur was formidable. He had taken down countless people and the fact that he's contained only makes him more dangerous. I pretend otherwise when I tell him my stories and deliver food, but Asterion is one that kills indiscriminately and without remorse. Theseus would have his hands full when he reached the center of the labyrinth.

"Not that becoming an Athenian queen wouldn't suit me," Phaedre continued, straightening her back. "It would bring our great kingdoms together. I would be the queen who brought peace. Perhaps if he succeeds Father will allow it." She smiled, as if this was the first time she'd thought of it.

"You know you can't trust him, right?" I responded, wondering what she promised him in return.

"What do you know about anything?"

"I know he's not in a position to make promises."

She huffed and rolled her eyes. "Well," she said, stroking the golden fabric, "It's not as if you're marrying anybody. Father made that clear." She shot me a pointed look.

I sighed, frustrated. Regardless of whether or not she went to Athens, she was right about marriage. She would become the queen of some distant land and I would remain here. I let that comment stretch out between us.

"At least I will have Thalia," I sighed. I didn't mean

to say it out loud.

Phaedre huffed. "Doubtful. Have you not seen where she spends her nights? It's only a matter of time before she ends up like the others."

I stopped. "What do you mean?"

Her eyes widened as she looked at me like I was an idiot. "Did you never wonder what happened to Bea? Or Raisa, that pretty little serving girl?"

I remembered Bea, who used to give us dancing lessons. When lessons stopped suddenly, I didn't think to question it or wonder why I never saw her again. To me, it meant more time outside or with Alcina. "No, what happened?"

She looked at me with the exaggerated patience of someone explaining something simple to a small child. "Honestly, you can be so dense sometimes. Our mother happened. Everyone knows not to cross her, especially with Father. Anyone he takes to his bed dies. It's only a matter of time."

My legs felt weak as the pieces came together. Encouraged by the stricken look on my face, she continued, "Raisa didn't even make it out of his room. They say he's cursed, that the very act kills them." She raised her eyebrows and paused to make sure I understood her lewd reference. "Raisa was barely recognizable, like she had been turned inside out. I don't know what kind of poison or sorcery she used, but- "

"Stop. You made your point." My chest so tight I

207

had to fight for breath.

Phaedre reached out and patted my arm, tilting her head in a smug gesture of sympathy, while hiding a faint smile. She knew the arrow she shot hit home. Having achieved her goal, she switched topics and kept chattering, but I didn't hear her. My head swam. I needed air. I threw my distaff down, said I wasn't feeling well and left without looking back.

It's Thalia, I told myself. She's different. After all, it's not like she had a choice. Knowing what she means to me, would my mother really harm her? I thought of my mother and her pride. Always the most beautiful woman in the room. Always in control. And then of Thalia with her large, almond shaped eyes, beautiful before she even knew it. I knew the answer, but I didn't want to acknowledge it. Thalia, my friend, was marked the first time my father called her to his bed. And there was nothing I could do about it.

~ 15 ~

I wandered the hallways trying to get Phaedre out of my head until I reached the courtyard where the Athenian children were playing a game, chasing each other and giggling. I stood on the sidelines, watching them play seemingly unaware that a monster lurked for them. They ran and jumped, tagged each other and ran away. I didn't understand the rules of their game, but their laughter made me smile until the knowledge of what was to come of them sank like poison into my chest. Still, I wanted to join them, to feel that security of youth, that feeling that everything would work out. At the same time, I wanted to hug them and spirit them away to a place where nothing would harm them.

Like a lightning bolt thrown by the God himself, I knew what I had to do.

I found him in the outdoor theater, sitting by himself in the top row looking down at the floor. Tomorrow, this theater would be packed with people, all cheering for the justice meted out by the Minotaur. Today, it was deserted, the empty seats glowed white in the bright sun. Standing there all alone, Theseus didn't look like a fierce warrior, grown hard by battle. He looked like maybe what he was, a guy about my age in a strange land surrounded by people who weren't his friends. He looked weary, perhaps a little sad.

That vulnerability disappeared when he saw me climbing the stairs. His face lost its shadows as he straightened his back and looked out over the floor, as if preparing to address the crowd. I kept moving forward, trying not to think about what I was doing. His gaze reminded me of the way a hawk watches a mouse.

"As I see it, you have two problems," I said.

"Just two?" he responded, amused.

"You'll be put into the labyrinth with no weapons. You'll have to kill him with your bare hands."

He chuckled. "So? I've killed bigger monsters than that."

"Really? Aster- I mean, the Minotaur, hasn't eaten all week, which means he's angry and hungry. On a good week, when he's well-fed and happy, he has

210

ripped apart men bigger than you." I shivered as I remembered the wreckage that has been pulled out of the labyrinth.

Theseus seemed to consider this, then shrugged his shoulders. "Don't underestimate me, Princess," he said. "How do you know I don't already have that covered?"

I watched him study me, his face sharp, his body relaxed. Was this what he asked of Phaedre? Did she agree to get a weapon into the labyrinth? I shook my head. That was ridiculous. Where would Phaedre get a weapon? Besides, even if she somehow got a sword, she would never set foot in the labyrinth. She could hardly hand him a sword on his way in. Still, the crown he dangled would motivate her and she was resourceful. The corner of his mouth curled up into a half-smile.

"Even so, you still have a second problem."

He raised his eyebrow. "Which is?"

"If you do manage to not die in there, you have to get out. Nobody has been able to find their way out."

"Nobody?"

"Nobody except for Daedalus, who built it. And me."

"You, Princess? Please," he scoffed.

"Yes. Me. Who do you think feeds him? I was taught by Daedalus himself years ago and now, I'm the only one who goes in and out. Me. Not Phaedre."

His posture stiffened. "What about the servants who

clean up after him?"

"I lead the guards in... and out."

His eyes narrowed, appraising what I said, and scoffed, "You're just a girl."

Now, I steeled myself and looked right into those unsettling blue eyes. "You underestimate me, Prince."

I struggled to maintain a blank exterior, but my insides were boiling. I couldn't believe I was out here talking to him like this, proposing what I was about to offer. He affected a look of indifference, but I knew I had his attention. His eyes, the color of a lazy summer sea, fixed on me with an expression of boredom and intensity. I wanted not to notice, but I could feel the warmth shoot through my body. Angry that I was letting him affect me, I willed myself to snap out of it. I refused to be the first one to look away. So, we were stuck, eyes locked for several moments.

"You never met my brother," I said. He shook his head.

"He was the pride of our island. My people feel his loss every day." My voice started to shake as Androgeos' face jumped into my memory, his smile shining as he swung me around.

"I have no quarrel with your brother or you, for that matter, but he has been avenged." He gestured to the palace. "Those kids did not kill your brother. They should not pay for a past they had no part in."

"I agree."

"You agree?" he said, raising his eyebrow in

212

surprise.

"Yes."

"So, you'll help me?"

"I cannot help you. I am a princess of Crete. I cannot defy my King and father. This is my home. If I help you, I lose everything."

"So, why are you here then?"

"I need you to take my maid with you. And her um.. husband."

"Why would I do this?"

"Because you claim to protect the innocent and they need protection."

"And what of you?" He stepped closer to me.

"What about me?"

"Do you also need protection?"

"No. I can protect myself."

"Hmm. Can you?" He said, stepping closer. Suddenly, I was very aware of how close we stood. Too aware.

"Yes." I held my ground.

"You have just told me I have no chance of finding my way out of the labyrinth. How do you propose I save your maid if I can't find my way out?"

I was prepared to draw him a map, but I realized with a start that it wouldn't be enough. It was foolish of me not to have thought this through before charging up here. I heard myself say, "If you save Thalia, I will help you."

"Princess. That is dangerous for you."

"Yes."

"If you help me, you could not stay here. I will take you back with me. My father will welcome you. You will be an honored guest in Athens."

"Not a guest. I've seen what happens to honored guests in Athens. If I help you, you will take me back as your wife." What was I saying? I should turn around and run back to the palace and forget this conversation. Yet, I couldn't. My voice was steady. It was so wrong, but I knew this was the way.

"My wife?" He studied me, thinking. "My wife."

"Yes. I will help you defeat the Minotaur and return to your family. As your wife, not as a princess of Crete."

It made me feel sick, but it was true. He was my solution. In one gesture, I would save Thalia and gain my freedom. But at the expense of my family. I thought of Asterion, who loved lavender. Of my beautiful island and all the people I love. Was I really going to sacrifice them for this? I also thought of the children, innocent of the crime they were paying for. Crete was better than that. We are an island of artists, not murderers. I could stop it. There was no future here, for Thalia or me. Phaedre would marry, Thalia would be gone, and I would be alone, either imprisoned here or sold in marriage to my uncle. The thought was a weight on my chest. I was suddenly burning up, and a little dizzy. I kept myself under control and looked at Theseus, waiting for his response. He studied me for a moment, as if considering his options, maybe trying to figure out if I was serious or not. Or more likely, which princess he wanted. After a few tense moments, a huge grin spread across his face.

"Yes. Beautiful Princess of Crete, you will be my wife. Our kingdoms will be united, the beast will be gone and there will be peace. We will end this."

I nodded. It was settled. "I will come by your quarters later on and we will talk of a plan." I didn't wait for a response. If I thought about it, I wouldn't even know if I could get to his quarters or which room was his. Details to figure out later. Without looking back, I spun around and ran down the stairs. What had I just done? I agreed to treason, to marry someone I didn't know, to help kill my half-brother, to save those children, to save Thalia. To be free. As I turned away, I couldn't shake the nagging feeling that Theseus had somehow just gotten exactly what he wanted. My heart raced. My face flushed. I ran across the theater floor and out of the theater and threw up all over a pink cluster of rock roses.

* * *

I didn't stop running until I could no longer feel Theseus' eyes on my back. Out of the corner of my eye, I saw someone duck into the storage area near the side entrance of the palace. Thalia. I followed her and when I saw her face, alive and unharmed, relief crashed over me. Before I knew it, I was crying and apologizing. We clung together and soon, we were both sniffling and interrupting each other, apologies tangled in worry.

"I should have known. I don't know how I couldn't," I started again.

"You wouldn't have." She tried to console me with a sympathetic look.

"You and I are different," Thalia said. "It doesn't seem like it, but we are. Our worlds are different."

"I should have known. But," I said, brightening. "I have a plan."

"What kind of plan? What did you do?" Her dark eyes narrowed.

I told her of my conversation with Theseus. She slumped down on one of the clay containers. "Are you crazy? You can't do that!"

"Yes, I can. It makes perfect sense. It's the only way."

"You will lose everything. If you do that, you can never come back here."

"I know."

"This is your home."

"I know."

"It's all you know."

"I know."

"You can't."

"I have to. You need to get away from here. I need

to get away from here. This is how we do it. Darius too. We have to go find him." I jumped up, but she grabbed my arm and pulled me back.

"Are you sure? You thought about this?"

"Yes. We'll be all right. Alcina, though. She'll be upset." I looked into her face, which was wet with tears. She pulled me in and hugged me tightly.

"She wants me to be safe. You are my family too. Besides, you're right. We have to go." she said.

I helped her gather jars of grains, spices and olive oil and we hurried off to the kitchens to drop them off. We had much to do. I told the cook that Thalia had an urgent errand to run and we headed off to the fields to find Darius.

We found him repairing a broken fence. As soon as she saw him, Thalia lit up and ran over to him. He swept her up and they huddled close together. I stayed behind, looking out over the fields, trying to give them privacy. Cattle lolled, with their giant doe eyes taking in everything around them. A calf bounced along behind them, nibbling on grass and trying to nudge his mom into play. She wasn't interested and kept eating grass and looking around.

As I watched the cows, I thought of Asterion in his prison, trapped between two worlds. Not human. Not an animal. A monster in between. I wondered what he would be like if he had been allowed to roam free. Would he have played with this calf? I shook my head. I remembered the stories of the mangled nurses,

217

who suffered for trying to care for him. Before being confined to the labyrinth, he left a trail of blood. No, he wouldn't have played with that calf. He would be more likely to slaughter it than play with it. Still, in all the time I'd been feeding him, he'd never once attacked me. It didn't matter, I decided. He was a monster. His path was one of fear and isolation.

I glanced over at Thalia and Darius with their heads together, wholly absorbed in each other. I liked the way her body relaxed around him, how her head tilted toward him when he talked. I wondered how much he knew and how much she would tell him. Anxious, I crossed my arms and kicked the dirt. It was late and I still had much to do. As if reading my thoughts, Thalia looked over and waved her hand. She kissed Darius on the cheek and ran over to me, her face bright and happy.

"He will meet us on the ship," she said. I nodded. Of course, he would follow her.

I squeezed Thalia's hand before she ran off to collect clothing and food to leave for him at the drop off point. The rest I needed to do alone. My first stop was the blacksmith's shop. Theseus was a warrior and an honored guest, but my father wasn't stupid. He stripped Theseus of his sword before allowing him off our ship the day he arrived and there was no sign of his famous copper club. Even though his reputation was formidable, he would need something other than his bare hands to take down the Minotaur.

I'd never been inside a blacksmith's shop and I didn't have time to change my clothes. I straightened my posture and entered the shop as myself, the Princess Ariadne. Inside the shop, the unmistakable smell of fire and metal greeted me. Spikes and tools of all sizes hung from the walls. It was dark and dirty, but warm. A young man, who must have been the blacksmith's apprentice banged on a piece of metal, which glowed red hot. It took him a minute to notice me and I watched him concentrating on his task, listening to the clank of the tools mold the metal into place. I was fascinated by the violence and the beauty. When he saw me, he stopped and rose to his feet.

With a warm smile, I nodded and greeted him. I told him I was there on behalf of my mother to collect the piece she commissioned for the tribute. His look of absolute confusion and panic made me feel guilty for my deception, but I pushed it away. I needed a weapon. After all, what use did a princess have for weaponry? He was understandably confused and scoured the shop for what I required. He apologized multiple times and explained that the master blacksmith was away on an errand, which was a relief as the master blacksmith would surely know my story was thin. When he couldn't find it, I suggested we look at what was already built to see if any of those would do. He had swords, knives and daggers of all sizes. I picked up a long knife and turned it over in my hand, admiring the craftsmanship. It was smooth

219

and sleek, engraved with double axes on the handle. I liked how solid it felt in my hands. I assured him that this knife would do perfectly and slipped a gold ring off my finger as payment. He looked at me sideways, but dropped the ring in his pocket and didn't ask further questions. I tucked the knife in my belt under my shawl and hurried away.

As I neared the labyrinth, I slowed my pace, trying to look casual and remain unseen. On most days, nobody came near it, but being so close to the tribute, servants bustled around and mischievous children dared each other to see who could get the closest. I pressed myself into the shadow of an alcove, watching a group of boys. One brave boy crept toward the outer wall of the labyrinth. He glanced back at his friends, took a deep breath and then jutted forward to touch the wall. For a brief second, he lingered there before turning and darting as fast as he could back to his circle. They enveloped him, egging on the next one. Without warning, they scattered like mice in the pantry.

I looked around to see what frightened them, but it was too late. My father had seen me. He came around the corner with his arms outstretched.

"Ariadne! What a surprise. Did you see those boys?" He chuckled, amused at their daring. At least he was in good spirits.

I bowed and straightened. "Father."

"What brings you out here?" he asked, embracing

me.

"I was just getting some air," I responded, pulling away, conscious of the weight of the knife under my belt and unable to look at him. Did he somehow know what I had done? I held my breath, waiting.

"I'm glad we ran into each other. Come. Walk with me."

I nodded and he led us back toward the theater. I bit my lip and nervously tugged at my shawl.

"Do you remember when you were a girl and the war began?"

"Of course, Father."

"All the men and boys volunteered, eager to avenge their prince. You grabbed a sword and tried to join the fighting lessons. Do you remember?"

I smiled. I did remember. We were not an island of warriors. We were craftsmen, artists, and fisherman. When the call came, the boys showed up in droves, but they needed instruction. Many didn't even know how to hold a sword, much less fight with one. They wanted to fight. So did I. When Androgeos didn't return, I wanted to be an Amazon and charge through Athens on my horse and bring him back. Make them pay for what they'd done.

"Of course, Father. I wanted to fight. To avenge Androgeos," I said.

He smiled. I noticed now how the crinkles in his eyes had deepened, how his hair was streaked with silver. "You weren't much bigger than the sword, but you held your ground. When I tried to drag you away, you kicked and screamed like an animal. So, I let you stay. Do you remember?"

"Yes."

How could I forget? After Androgeos' murder, my mother didn't come out of her room for weeks. Alcina was busy with Phaedre and Thalia, who were little. Everything was chaos. During those weeks, I was my father's child. Being outside, swinging that sword and coming back sweaty and dirty, we had a single purpose. It was one of my best childhood memories hand in hand with my worst.

"You were so mad when I wouldn't let you on a ship to sail to Athens." He chuckled at the memory. "Child, I know you love Crete. I never *doubt* that." He put his arm around me again, clasping my shoulder.

"Thank you." I wondered where he was going with this.

"You were so little. You probably don't remember, but most of those boys didn't come home. On both sides."

"I know, Father. Why are you telling me this?"

"At the banquet, I saw how you watched the tribute. You have a warrior's spirit, but a mother's conscience."

"It just seems sad. None of them have anything to do with what happened to Androgeos."

"Yes, but it's their duty to fulfill Athens' debt to us. No more war in exchange for the tribute. That was the deal we struck. It's important to remember. War has a price, but so does peace. Unfortunately, the young always seem to be the ones who pay it, but it's the way it is. The tribute ended the war. Without it, we would have destroyed Athens. Those same children could die in battle. More children would die in war. Athens knows it too. That's why we have the treaty. It served both our ends. Our Androgeos is avenged and Athens remains. It keeps the peace."

"Yes, Father. I understand."

"I know it's been difficult for you. This marriage uncertainty. We don't fully understand that prophesy yet. We just need to be safe until we understand."

"Yes, Father, but what of Calix? Are you considering my uncle's proposal?"

"My brother is ambitious. He oversteps, but what he suggests might be a solution to the prophecy. Regardless of our past or how he feels about me, he would not harm Crete. That's what we have to protect." Yes, I thought, but what about protecting me?

"After the tribute, we will visit the oracle and see if it is favorable." He bent down and kissed my forehead, signaling that the matter was closed.

He left me overlooking the bay, the knife burning at my side. I stood there for a while, feeling the breeze on my face and looking out over the water. Theseus' ship bobbed in the water, it's black sails like an omen. Perhaps my father was right and the tribute was necessary to maintain balance and safety. What would happen if Theseus was successful? Would my father launch ships to seek revenge? The war would be my fault. I saw in my mind the burning shore from the prophecy. But, what if the war had already started? What if they sent Theseus ahead of time and the Athenian warships were already on their way? Then, another thought crept in. What if Theseus failed? In helping him, I will be a traitor. If he fails, I would have no way off the island. I needed to talk to Theseus. Maybe there is another way. If my father is open to marriage with my uncle, perhaps we can talk to him and present another option.

These thoughts tumbled over each other in my mind as I walked back. I no longer knew what was right. I was so lost in my mind, I almost bumped into Alcina, who rushed up to me waving her arms.

"Ariadne! Where have you been? I've been looking everywhere for you." She looked frantic.

"What's wrong?"

"It's Thalia. She's gone."

"What do you mean, gone? I just saw her."

"She's gone. I looked all over, including the storerooms and the kitchen. She's nowhere to be found. None of the servants have seen her either."

My heart started to pound. I wanted to reassure Alcina, to offer reason and tell her everything would be all right. Thalia was probably gathering supplies or making last-minute plans with Darius, but the plan had to be secret. I couldn't tell her. If she knew, she would be treasonous too and I couldn't have that on my conscience. Alcina looked like a rabbit in a trap. Her panic infected me and I couldn't stop the worry from creeping into my belly. I hugged her tightly and told her not to worry, we would find her. Alcina's familiar scent of soap and lemons calmed me a bit and I pulled away. She gave me a hard look and something unspoken passed between us. What if I was too late and my mother already got to her? We decided to split up.

Alcina returned to check inside and I walked around the outside, toward the labyrinth. The entrance was empty now and I saw my opportunity. If anyone saw me, I would say I thought I saw someone enter and I wanted to make sure nobody was in danger. With those boys playing around here, nobody would question that.

After looking around, I slid into the entrance. The air in the labyrinth was still. Nothing moved. No matter how often I've been inside, the stillness always surprised me. After a few turns, I pulled the knife out of my belt and placed it in the corner. I didn't need to bother hiding it. The guards might peek their heads in, but nobody would come this far in. With that done, I turned around and walked back to the entrance. After stopping to make sure nobody was there, I slipped back outside.

"My Princess, what are you doing?"

My head whipped around to see Dionysus casually leaning against the wall of the labyrinth. All traces of the sadness I glimpsed the night before were gone. Instead, amusement played on his face.

"What are you doing here? You shouldn't be here," I said.

"I wanted to see you. Come. Walk with me." He held out his hand.

I glanced around. We were alone. My gaze landed on his eyes, glinting like fire. I took his hand and set off beside him down the path. For a while, neither of us spoke. In the distance, a bird chirped. He stared straight ahead.

"You were right," he said.

"About what?"

"In the woods. The angry husband. I shouldn't have done that."

"No, you shouldn't have. You could have stopped it."

"I know. I'm sorry."

"It's not me you should apologize to."

He sighed. "This isn't going well."

"What's not going well? What are you talking about?" I stopped to face him. A breeze rustled the tall grass, stirring my dress.

"I want you to come with me."

"What?"

"I see what you are doing. This is a dangerous game to play. I can protect you. Come with me."

I yanked my hand free. "Protect me? From what?"

"Yourself. Theseus is not the way."

"I don't need your protection. I can take care of myself." I paused. "Besides, I think you have enough women followers for your temple."

He sighed and raked a hand through his hair. "This isn't what I meant to say."

"What did you mean to say? I don't understand."

"You aren't like anybody I've ever met. You are fearless. And beautiful. I can be reckless, but not about this. About you. I've helped countless farmers in every country, but it's all been empty – until you shared it with me at Mandilari's farm. You make me want to be better. Come. We can spread that happiness everywhere. Be by my side."

My mouth dropped open as I stared at him, shocked.

"But, you're a god," I said.

"Half god," he corrected.

The vulnerability on his face softened me, but I thought of his mortal mother, burned alive by Zeus' full light. The problem was when I looked at him, I didn't see the god. I saw the man, earnest and flawed, with a lopsided smile and reckless hair. He closed the space between us and my heart pounded. I ripped my eyes away from him.

"I'm just a mortal. It can't work. Look at what happened to your mother."

"I am not my father," he breathed, teeth clenched,

eyes blazing.

"And I am not some silly girl, dazzled by a handsome face and a glass of wine."

He grinned. "You think I'm handsome."

"That's not the point."

"What is the point?"

I laid my hands on his chest and pushed him away. "I'm sorry. I can't deal with this right now. I have to go."

I left him standing in the path as I ran back up the hill. Every instinct I had called me to look back, but I didn't. I couldn't. If I did, I might not have kept going. I didn't want to see his face or feel his eyes on me. My decision was made and my course set in motion. I only hoped it was the right one.

~ 16 ~

The sunset burned up the sky in a riot of orange and purple, but it felt hollow. I couldn't take my eyes off the children as the guards led them from the theater to the sanctuary for cleansing. With their wide eyes, fearful expressions and gray pallor, they looked like ghosts. How could this be the path to peace?

My father strode forward to address the crowd, cutting off their cheers to an expectant hush. His speech was a slow burn about the greatness of Crete and our mercy with Athens. At its crescendo, he introduced the tribute, and the crowd rose to its feet applauding our greatness. The tribute, he said, was a renewal, an act of good faith that ensured our continued peace with Athens. I fidgeted in my seat. Next to me, Phaedre wore a fixed smile, but her eyes never left Theseus, standing protectively between the crowd and the children.

After he finished, my mother rose, pausing as all eyes settled on her. A murmur of confusion rippled through the room and even my father looked first surprised and then concerned. It was unusual for my mother to speak at an assembly and even more unprecedented for her to do it without my father's blessing. From the look on his face, he wasn't pleased. With a wave of her hand, two servants stepped forward. I gasped. Thalia stood between them. In chains. My mother announced there was a last-minute addition to the tribute and the guards pushed Thalia forward. She fell to her knees in front of my family. When she looked up, her face was a mask of terror. Her wild eyes darted from my mother to me and back again. My heart thumped in my chest. What was going on? Thalia was supposed to be on the ship. My father stared straight ahead, teeth clenched, face hard.

"This girl," my mother started, sweeping her hand toward Thalia, "has grown up in my own house, under my care. Like an asp in a house of doves. Assigned as a maid to Princess Ariadne, your heir to the throne, she had all of my trust and full access to the palace. I loved her as one of my own, and her betrayal leaves me with a heavy heart." She paused here, the picture of sadness and innocence.

"Don't be fooled by her pitiful appearance. This girl committed treason of the highest order. She tried to take something that doesn't, and will never, belong to her." She paused here, giving Thalia a withering look. Thalia stared at the ground.

"We are a house of mercy, of learning and strength, but we don't tolerate threats against our people or to our rule, even from those closest to us. I don't enjoy sentencing her, but her sacrifice will bring favor. What a better tribute to the gods than one of youth and beauty?" The crowd cheered. She smiled and continued, "As always, I do what is necessary to protect Crete."

My father turned pale, but his expression didn't change. Why didn't he stop this? This was his fault. I willed him to stand and do what's right. He never met my eyes or glanced at Thalia. He wasn't going to do anything.

With that, the bottom fell out of my stomach. My resolve hardened. Thalia joined the tributes and my father signaled it was time to proceed to the sanctuary. Rage flooded my body, my hands balled into fists. Everything went rigid. This wasn't about treason or Crete or even paying tribute to the gods. This was about revenge. My mother was using Thalia as Dionysus used Pentheus. To set an example. Thalia wasn't like the others. She grew up in the palace. Slept in my quarters. My mother knew what she meant to me and it didn't matter. I meant nothing. It wasn't

231

enough to keep me here, unwed and shut away or sell me in marriage to someone twice my age. They needed to also deprive me of my only friend? For an offense that wasn't her fault?

My legs shook with such ferocity, I didn't know how I would walk. Even after Phaedre told me of my mother's malice, there was a part of me that didn't believe she would harm Thalia. How wrong I was. I fought to keep my emotions off my face and my breathing steady. The plan could not fail.

I felt Phaedre take my hand and I gripped it for strength. She leaned over and whispered, "You still have me."

My hand lay lifeless in hers. With the priestess and my parents leading the way, we left the theater and headed to the small sanctuary to purify the sacrifice. It was like walking in a nightmare.

The Priestess of Poseidon's temple was striking, with a gentle smile and a rhythmic sway. I watched her glide forward, with her elaborate headdress floating overhead and thought she looked like a goddess herself. I kept glancing behind, but Thalia wouldn't acknowledge me. She trudged forward, staring at the ground. In their crisp white tunics, the Athenian children trailed behind her, faces forward and expressions blank.

Theseus brought up the rear with the swagger of a conquering hero rather than someone being marched to a gruesome death. I searched his face for signs of nervousness, but I found none. He actually winked at me before raising his arm to wave at the crowd. It was appalling. I wished for a moment of his confidence. Since we hadn't spoken after forming our alliance, I would have to trust he would find the weapon I left unless I could speak to him somehow. Sweat rolled down my back. Beside me, Phaedre gripped my hand and dragged me forward. Rather than the triumph I expected to see on her face, I saw concern. In that moment, I was thankful for her. I don't think I could have walked without her steady hand pulling me forward. My hand was limp, but she never let go. She held me up.

Outside the sanctuary, the Priestess lit a fire and burned a blend of rosemary, thyme and sage, purifying the air and sending smoke to the gods. She said a prayer and then it was time for the cleansing. As the royal family, we followed her into the small room, but nobody else was allowed in for this sacred ritual. It was a small rectangular room with a clay tub in the center. Paintings celebrating the harvest and the sea decorated the walls. My favorite showed a group of children picking wild celery, a plant sacred to Poseidon. I always liked its bright colors and the happiness of the scene, but now it felt hollow. We pressed into the back as, one by one, the children were brought forward to the priestess. She greeted each with an invocation to Poseidon. Then, taking each by the hand, led them to the basin, where she washed their faces, hands and feet and anointed them with oils. To finish, the priestess placed a wreath of wild celery, ivy and flowers on their heads as she chanted the sacred words. They were now pure for the gods.

When Thalia was led in, it took all my self-control not to run to her and shield her from the priestess. My heart pounded. She shuffled forward, shoulders slumped, staring at her feet. After what my family had done to her, I couldn't blame her. I wanted to grab her, to tell her that she could count on me. That I would fix it, but I didn't. I knew I already failed her. As with the others, the priestess dribbled water over Thalia's collar bones and wiped away her impurities. When she was finished, she rubbed a few drops of oil into her temples and Thalia joined the others outside the sanctuary. As she walked past, my mother straightened her back and stared straight ahead.

After the cleansing, I felt dirty. The gods demanded sacrifice, but it was supposed to be a gift, a token of respect and gratitude. When you slaughter a goat for a feast, the gods share in the meat. The goat is blessed, his energy lives on. This was different. These were children. It was Thalia. This was blood and vengeance. Instead of a proper burial, they would be wrapped in the shroud we spent months weaving and burned under the guise of piety, turned to smoke and ash like any common farm animal. This was wrong.

With the purification complete, we set out on the

final leg of the procession, which ended at the entrance of the labyrinth. By now it was almost dark and servants held torches to light the way. At this point, even Theseus had lost his swagger. Like the others, he walked forward in silence. At the entrance, the tribute lined up and the priestess blessed them again, blessed Crete and then blessed the Minotaur. My father stepped forward and thanked them for their sacrifice and spoke again about the continued peace between our two great nations. The words ran together.

My father stood beaming next to me. When he put his hand on my shoulder, I twisted out of his grasp and turned to face him.

"Father. I need a moment to say goodbye." Anger had made me bold. For once, I didn't ask for permission. He nodded.

Relieved, I exhaled some of the tension, my mind racing. I wouldn't look at my mother.

Shaking free of Phaedre, I ran forward to Thalia, pulling her into a hug. A guard twitched forward, but my father stayed him with a slight movement of his hand. A single tear started to swell, but I pushed it away and kissed both her clammy cheeks. As I did, I whispered "Don't worry. I'll get you out." A flicker of recognition flashed across her eyes, but she did not acknowledge it. I went through the whole line, kissing each child on each cheek. I had no words for them. I couldn't imagine the terror they felt at being led into the labyrinth in the dark. Their faces were blank. Theseus was the last one in the line and the one closest to the entrance.

As I stood before him, locked into those blue eyes, which appeared gray in the light. I said something meaningless and as I kissed his cheek, I pulled a spool of Phaedre's golden thread out of the folds of my dress and slipped it onto the back of his belt. I kept hold of the string. As I kissed his other cheek, I whispered, "Check the first bend. Don't forget Thalia. Follow the string out."

His skin was hot and smelled of lavender oil and sweat. Like the others, he stood still, but his eyes followed me as I walked to the entrance. I took my place at the door with my hands behind my back. Shaking, I hooked the thread around a notch in the doorway. I looked around, nervous that someone had seen me or had noticed the thin line between Theseus' belt and the doorway. I held my breath, waiting to hear the angry boom of my father's voice, but there was nothing. With a final blessing, the guards prodded the group into the labyrinth. A bolt slid across the door. Now, all I could do was wait.

SHIP 3

Once the thick wooden door closed on the labyrinth, the crowd dissipated. There would be nothing to see tonight. Nobody runs headlong into the middle of the labyrinth. They hover around the edges, thinking they can find a way out, a weakness in the design, but it's designed to keep them inside. Every step unbalances their sense of direction and draws them closer to the middle. Sometimes, there is nothing more terrifying than silence and the labyrinth has silence to spare. In the dark, guided by fear, the tributes would stumble into the Minotaur. Afterward, the crowd would gather to gawk at the bloody remains brought out to be burned and offered up to the gods. If it takes longer than one night, guards would be sent in to prod them forward. This has never happened. People always think they will be the one to survive. Theseus will no doubt run headlong into the center. Until then, guards listen for the shrieks and screams that signal the end. But, tonight, we feasted.

The sacrifice, as a gesture of new beginnings, always happened on the night of the equinox, the time of balance when night and day are equal. It was a time sacred to our gods. To honor them, we have a feast to celebrate the abundance of the summer harvest before performing the sacrifice to appease the gods and honor the treaty with Athens. So, while the tribute struggled in the labyrinth, the palace was alight with torches, musicians and food. Thanks to the work of Dionysus, wine also flowed freely.

I leaned against a fountain, watching my father's advisers and the important people in town mill about toasting their good fortune. The wine sloshing in their glasses made me think of Dionysus and I wondered where he was. I looked for him in the red, smiling faces of the courtiers and in the corners of the courtyard, but he wasn't there. Was I wrong to send him away? I remembered his face, so full of mischief. Was that love I saw? In my core, I didn't believe he would hurt me. He'd shown me magic and beauty, and encouragement.

My fingers tapped and tugged at my skirt. Did I make a terrible mistake? I pushed those thought away. It didn't matter now. My choice was made and I needed to see it through. My eyes darted around the courtyard, which was full of people, men and women alike, laughing over bites of food lifted from platters and servants refilling glasses. Notes from the lute lingered overhead.

Every year, I looked forward to the annual harvest celebration, but tonight, I paced the courtyard worried about what was happening in the labyrinth. Did Darius make it to the ship? Did Thalia tell Theseus of our plan? Smells trailing behind heaping plates of food made my mouth water, but when I tried to eat, every mouthful turned to sludge. Anxiety coiled my gut into a knot. I sipped a glass of wine, hoping it would calm me, but it curdled in my stomach.

I circled the courtyard a few times, stopping to make polite conversation with some of the ladies of the court. Lady Ionia, the tiresome wife of my father's chief adviser, gripped my arm, holding me close as she prattled on about her daughter's upcoming marriage. I nodded politely and made all the correct responses, but I wasn't listening. My attention was on Phaedre beelining toward me. I extricated myself from Lady Ionia, promising to stop by later to continue our conversation when Phaedre hooked my arm and pulled me into a dark alcove. She pressed a small vial into my hand.

"If you are going to save her, you'll need this," she

said.

I searched her face for signs of deception or malice, but found none. She cocked her head. "For the guards," she added, as if I was dense.

My fingers closed around the pouch. "Why are you doing this? You hate Thalia."

"I don't hate Thalia. Besides, you're my sister. That's all I ever wanted." She shook her head. "It doesn't matter. Whatever is between us, I don't want you to get caught. You can stop looking at me like you don't know what I'm talking about. We both know you're going in to save her."

I didn't deny it.

"What is it?"

"It will just make them sleep, nothing else."

"Are you sure?"

"Yes. I'm not a fool." She narrowed her eyes, insulted at my suggestion that she didn't know her herbs. After all, we both learned from our mother.

I hesitated, not sure if I could trust her. In the end, I knew she was right and I didn't have much of a choice. My window to save Thalia shrank by the minute and in my hasty plan, I hadn't considered the guards. I hugged Phaedre, holding her close, wishing things were different between us, hoping I could trust her.

"Tomorrow, he will walk free from the labyrinth and ask Father for my hand."

"Theseus?"

"Who else?"

And there it was. Theseus. I nodded, unsure of what to say.

"He promised this?"

"Yes. Tomorrow, he will walk free and we will be together."

I smiled, comforted by her transparency.

"And that's why you're helping me? To help him get out?"

She tossed her hair. "No. I'm helping you because you're my sister. Theseus doesn't need my help. He does just fine on his own and besides, the guards will let him out tomorrow."

"And he wants to marry you?"

"He loves me."

"He just met you."

"He says that we will bring peace to our kingdoms." She held her hand over her heart. "Finally, a queen."

"Of Athens."

"A queen."

"Father will kill him."

"He won't. He'll see this is the only way."

I sighed and hugged my sister again. Tomorrow, depending on which promise Theseus kept, one of us would be disappointed. And I might be in the dungeon for treason. I forced a smile.

"Thank you, Phaedre. I truly wish you every happiness."

She beamed back at me and squeezed my hand

before slipping out of the shadows. I watched her glide back to the crowd, easily absorbed into their fold. The light from the lanterns gave her a golden glow and she radiated happiness. Always sure of her place, my beautiful sister would make an excellent queen. I only hoped that Theseus kept his promise to take Thalia and me off the island. Whatever happened after that, I would figure it out.

If Theseus walked out of the labyrinth tomorrow in front of an audience, my father would be furious. It meant he would have been bested by his enemy in front of his whole kingdom. Could Theseus really be that besotted with Phaedre that he would forget something this important? I hoped not. Killing the Minotaur was one thing. Getting out of the labyrinth was another. It wouldn't take much for my father to figure out who helped him escape. Phaedre was foolish if she thought our father would agree to terms with Theseus, but if anyone could get him to consider it, it would be her.

With a deep breath, I slid out of the alcove and took two wine glasses from a passing servant, ducked into a dark corner behind a statue and emptied the tincture into the glasses. Keeping to the shadows, I left the party and headed outside to the entrance of the labyrinth. I held out the wine to the guards on duty.

"You are missing all the fun," I said, trying to sound light and casual. These were two men from my father's guard and they didn't respond. I couldn't blame them. It was highly unusual for me to engage my father's guards in conversation, let alone bring them beverages.

"You must be thirsty," I said, holding out the wine, offering what I hoped was a playful smile.

They took the wine, but they didn't drink any and they didn't say anything. Apparently, I was terrible at flirting. How did Phaedre do this so well? I took a different tactic.

"I know I shouldn't be here. I'm just worried about Thalia." I widened my eyes and lowered my head. "Have you heard anything… from in there?"

The bigger guard shook his head and said gently, "No, Lady. It's been quiet."

I sighed.

"Can I-" I moved toward the door, but they each took a step, blocking the way.

"Sorry, Princess. We can't let you in. Nobody goes in or out."

"I understand. I'm just so worried…"

The bigger guard gave me a weak smile and tilted his head. "I know, Lady. It will all be over soon."

I nodded and turned around, slunk back to the party.

When I returned an hour later, the wine glasses laid empty and the guards were asleep, slumped over and leaning against the wall on either side of the door. I checked them and was relieved to see they were breathing.

I sat down against the door between them and listened for any sign of what was happening inside. Nothing. Just the uneven sound of my breath as I fought to control my breathing and tried to get lost in the stars overhead. The full moon hung bright in the sky, bathing everything in a cool, silver light. After a while, I stood to stretch my legs and stared at the door, willing Thalia and Theseus to burst through. Then I saw it. The notch where I tied the golden thread was empty. The string that was supposed to guide Theseus, Thalia and all of the children out of the labyrinth was gone. They were trapped.

I scanned the area to see if anyone was watching. It was empty in all directions, which wasn't very surprising. Nearly the whole village showed up to cheer as the people entered the labyrinth, but without the safety of a crowd, nobody would come near it. The simple bar across the outside was enough to keep it secure. After all, nobody wanted to go in and once they were in, nobody came out. Until today, hopefully.

I didn't relish the idea of wandering through the labyrinth in the dark, but I had no choice. If they were going to get out, I had to go in. I took a deep breath and eased the locking board out of place and pushed the heavy door open a sliver. A torch hung on the outer wall. I grabbed it and stepped into the darkness as the door clunked shut behind me. My heart pounded, but I crept forward, putting one foot in front of the other, trusting they knew the way. The flame, swallowed by the dark corners, threw ominous shadows, which could have hidden anything. I inched forward.

I concentrated on my footsteps and used them to steady my breathing like I did each time I entered to feed Asterion. Dark or light, I could do this. After a few turns, I heard the scuff and whimper of children. Relief washed over me when I saw them huddled together right where I left the knife. They were alive. Thalia flew into me, embracing me in a hug that almost knocked me over.

"Is everyone all right?" I asked, searching her face. She was pale and shaky, but otherwise unharmed.

She nodded. "Yes. He stayed with us for a while, until we couldn't hear talking outside anymore and then left. He found the knife." Thank the goddess. I felt my body relax and took her hands.

"What are you doing here? Is something wrong? Where's Darius?" Thalia asked, shaky and panicked.

I had forgotten about Darius. I shook my head, trying not to be annoyed. "Darius? No, he's fine, I'm sure. Hopefully, he's waiting on the ship. The thread came undone. I need to find Theseus. Without it, he won't find his way back."

She pointed in the direction he had taken. It was hard to leave Thalia and the kids alone in the dark, but I couldn't delay any longer. Theseus might be injured or lost and I needed to find him. Every moment counted, and we needed to get out of here.

After hugging Thalia and promising to be careful, I started after him. I kept my hand on the wall and the torch in the air and moved forward. I wove around corners and down familiar hallways and soon passed into the underground area, where darkness choked me, unbroken except from the light of my torch. Wherever Theseus was, he was in the dark. I hoped he was alone.

I heard him before I saw him. A snuffle and then a snort, a leg stomping the ground. Not knowing what to expect, I held my breath and rounded the corner. Theseus crouched low, ready to pounce. Once protected by the darkness, he was now illuminated by my torch. Our eyes locked together, confusion and then alarm flashing in his face. The Minotaur fixed his eyes on him, his face contorted in rage, his mouth snarling like he could breathe fire. His nostrils flared, he lowered his head and bellowed. It was a sound like no other. A sound of fury and pain.

Theseus jumped up, knife ready and ran at the Minotaur, who lowered his head, pointing his massive horns at him. Theseus lunged and thrust the blade, but the beast easily dodged the blow and charged. With a flick of his head, he picked Theseus up in his massive horns and flung him into the air. Theseus landed hard on the ground with a dull thud. I flinched and jerked forward and stopped. I couldn't help him. The Minotaur was on him in an instant, standing on Theseus' chest, crushing him into the ground. He screamed in pain as the Minotaur pounced down on him again.

I screamed for them to stop, and for a moment, they both turned to stare at me. For that flash of a second, the Minotaur was Asterion again. Confusion passed across his face and then disappeared. It was just a moment, but it was enough. Theseus struggled to get his breath back, but managed to scramble to his feet. With a ragged breath, he flew at the Minotaur, punching and kicking in a frenzy. The two clashed, fighting to stay alive in the darkness.

Saliva dripped from the Minotaur's jaws as he shook off the blows. Theseus slashed while the Minotaur growled and lunged at him with his sharp horns. I couldn't tell if the guttural growls were coming from Theseus or the Minotaur. Both were bloodied and sweaty and panting. I stood by, helpless as they fought, locked in an entangled knot of flailing limbs. The Minotaur fought like a scared animal, not a predator. He bared his teeth and growled and threw his body at Theseus who fell backward. The Minotaur pounced, trapping him on the ground and locking his hands around his neck. Theseus struggled, crushed under his weight.

"Get up, Theseus!" I screamed. He pulled a leg free, which loosened the Minotaur's grip, and caught his horns. He kept shaking the Minotaur's head from side to side, each time gaining strength and momentum. Then, gathering all his power, Theseus wrenched the horns all the around. There was a horrible snapping sound like a thick tree branch cracking, as the Minotaur's neck broke. He gurgled his last breath before flopping over limp, landing right on top of Theseus.

I bolted forward to help pull Theseus out. When he was free, he collapsed onto the floor, exhausted. I looked at Asterion beside him, limp with his head bent at an unnatural angle. This was the closest I had ever gotten to him. I ran my hand over his brow and down his cheeks. I closed his eyes. To my surprise, his fur was soft. Had he ever known a kind touch? Maybe when he was a baby, I thought. Seeing his calm face, I felt the height of my betrayal. He trusted me. Shame rose up inside me, making my breath catch. For years, I was the only person he knew. I fed him. I talked to him. Now, I had led this warrior to kill him.

Theseus, his strength gathered, took my hand and pulled me up from the floor. My body trembled and I felt heavy and sick. Without a word, he limped over to the Minotaur and took the knife from his belt. With two swipes, Theseus cut off Asterion's head. I screamed in horror and fell back to the ground.

He crouched in front of me and put his hands on each side of my face and brushed the hair out of my eyes. I recoiled from him, shaking and trembling. I couldn't take my eyes off Asterion's lifeless body, his blood soaking into the dirt. Theseus turned my face to look into his eyes. "Ariadne. The people must see that it's dead."

I nodded, but couldn't speak. My mind knew the truth of this, but my heart was broken. The rusty stench of blood and sweat hung thick all around us. We sat together in silence for a moment and I tried to focus on Theseus and not the bloodied mess behind me. Taking the horn of the severed head in one hand and my limp hand in the other, Theseus pulled me back up to standing. "Come. We must go."

Barely breathing, I led him through the twists and turns of the labyrinth. It was lucky my feet knew the path to take because my brain swirled. Instinct took over. When we reached the place where everyone awaited us, Thalia jumped up from the floor, where she was sitting in a circle with the children, the youngest on her lap. She must have been telling them stories. As soon as they saw Theseus, they rushed him, but stopped dead when they noticed the head dangling from his arm. They gaped at the head. One screamed. Somehow, he was able to calm them down and get them lined up. How he was able to inspire trust while holding a severed head was both annoying and astonishing. With Theseus bringing up the rear, we shuffled our way back through the final turns to the exit.

At the exit, I pushed on the door. It didn't budge. Panic swelled as I threw my body into it, but it still wouldn't open. Someone had slid the lock back in place. My shoulder throbbed, but I ignored it, slamming my body over and over into the door. We needed to get out. Theseus moved me aside and battered the door, but it still didn't budge. I spun around wildly, heart racing, trying to think of a way out. My father couldn't find me in here. Panic choked me. I would lose everything. It would all be for nothing. Some of the children started to cry, and Thalia murmured words of comfort. Then, I heard movement on the other side of the door. I motioned for everyone to be quiet.

"Hello? This is Princess Ariadne. Is someone there? Please let me out." I pounded on the door. I didn't have to fake the fear in my voice.

After several moments of silence, I heard shuffling outside the door and then the scraping of the wood being slid out of the lock. Please don't let it be my father, I thought. Finally, the door opened.

"Princess Ariadne? What are you doing in he-"

Theseus jumped forward, grabbed the guard and drew his knife across his throat. The man gasped, clutching his bloody neck and fell backward, just missing one of the unconscious guards on the ground. My hands flew to my own throat, as his blood emptied onto the dirt. So much blood. I added his death to the tally of my betrayals. What had I done?

We needed to get to the safety of the ships. Taking a deep breath, I stepped forward, gulping the clean

251

night air, grateful to be out of the labyrinth. We ushered the children out first and Thalia ran off with them, leading them toward the sea. Theseus closed the door, secured the lock and placed the Minotaur's head on the dead guard's stomach. I glanced at it one last time, whispered an apology, and then raced for the ships.

~ 18 ~

The full moon lit the path as we charged forward. My feet pounded the ground, sometimes getting tangled in the brush, but I kept running, trying to catch up to Thalia and the children. When I realized there was nobody next to me, I spun around to see Theseus standing in the path, facing back toward the palace. What was he doing? Was he going back to Phaedre like he'd promised her? Already shaky, I stepped toward him, but stopped when I noticed he wasn't moving. Still and focused, he was peering into the darkness of the brush, ready to pounce. Now I heard the rustling too. Footsteps.

A figure shot out of the brush and ran toward us.

Theseus lunged after him, tackling him to the ground. They hit with a thud and a groan and then tumbled together in a ball of fists. I bolted forward just in time to see Theseus pulling his knife out, straddling Darius in the dirt.

"No!"

They both stopped and Theseus looked at me, confused. "Darius," I said. "He's with us."

With a wary sigh, Theseus put the knife away and rolled off Darius. As they stood, relief washed over me as I gulped air trying to steady my heartbeat. They stood locked on to each other, each unsure of the other. The way they sized each other up reminded me of two wolves circling. Darius bowed, pledged to help us. With a nod, Theseus accepted. We needed to move on. Time was running out. Soon, someone would notice the fallen guards.

In shaky line, we pressed on down the path. Stones crunched under our feet as we shuffled along the rugged ground, trying to keep a good pace while staying quiet. In the dark, familiar things seemed frightening. The tangle of dark tree branches resembled guards and I heard footsteps in every rustle of leaves. Each shadow made me jump. My breath came ragged. Up ahead, I heard the crunch of someone stomping through the brush. Thalia flew up the path and threw herself at Darius. She clung to him and pointed up ahead where the children huddled together in a fork in the path, unsure which way to take.

With Darius and Thalia at the front and Theseus and me bringing up the rear, we set off down the path toward the shore. In the distance, the lonely phew of the scops owl broke the night air. I paused for a moment, waiting for the answering call of its mate. Nothing. Just the sigh of the wind and the crinkle of grass underfoot. It sounded ominous, that lonely call in the dark. Poor guy, I thought. I hope he finds his mate.

Theseus stopped short, making me stumble into him. He turned around, studying the darkness behind us. I didn't see anything, but a prickle of unease crept up the back of my neck. I started to ask Theseus what he heard, when an arrow whizzed past my head.

"Get down!" Theseus yelled. Up ahead, a child screamed. Darius flew forward, shaking off Thalia's hand as she tried to stay him. Theseus and Darius charged toward the direction of the arrow. I crouched down, panic rising.

One after another, arrows shot out of the darkness, either sailing past us or sticking into the ground. I spun around wildly, but I couldn't see anyone in the trees. Thalia came up next to me and gripped my hand. Down the path, Theseus and Darius fought with a guard in the brush. They grunted and punched, scraping the ground and rolling around in the dirt. The children crouched on the path ahead, terrified and frozen in place. It wasn't far to the beach.

255

We coaxed the children up and pointed to the shore.

"It's a race. Whoever gets there first wins. Run!"

They took off, scrambling toward the sea. Not wanting to leave Darius, Thalia started toward where the men were fighting. I scrambled after her.

"He's up there," Theseus called out, pointing to a little overhang beside a large, craggy oak tree. Darius bolted up the side of the hill.

The man at Theseus' feet was dead, his face bloody. He plucked the sword off the dead guard and held it out to me. I closed the distance between us and took the sword. It was heavy and awkward, a man's sword, not like the wooden sword I played with as a child.

"Go to the ship. We'll meet you there." He took off after Darius.

Thalia didn't budge. I grabbed her arm, trying to pull her along. "He'll be fine. We need to go. There are probably more guards coming. We need to get out of here." She stared ahead, watching the darkness that enveloped Theseus and Darius.

I yanked her forward. "Come. We must go!"

I pulled Thalia along as we shuffled over the path toward the shore. The sword hung awkwardly from my side, scraping the ground. Up ahead, a lump blocked the path. With horror, I recognized the white of the ceremonial robe. It was one of the children. Heart racing, we ran ahead to where a little girl was laying in the path, an arrow sticking through her shoulder. She was alive, but terrified and whimpering. I crouched down next to her and smoothed her hair. Guilt stabbed me because I worried about how this would slow us down.

"It's all right. We're here. What's your name?"

She looked at me, eyes wide and blurred with tears. She didn't respond.

"It's all right. It's going to be all right." I repeated it like a mantra. Maybe one of us would believe it. My mind whirled. My first thought was that we needed to get her to my mother, but that was stupid. Thalia and I would have to handle it. Right now, we were all she had. Next to me, Thalia studied her shoulder, deep in thought. I tried to gather the girl in my arms, but she screamed in pain when her shoulder was jostled.

"I've got you. It's just a little bit to the ship." Her eyes stared back at me, round with terror. I smoothed her hair, trying to offer comfort and distract her from Thalia, who grabbed the shaft of the arrow.

"I'm sorry, little one," Thalia said and snapped off the sharp end of the arrow. The girl screamed. Blood poured out of the wound where it was jostled. I took off my shawl and wrapped it around her narrow shoulders, trying to pack the wound and support the arrow shaft. Thalia and I lifted her up.

"I know it hurts, but we need to get to the ship. Then, you can rest and we'll take care of your shoulder. Do you understand?" I said.

257

The girl nodded and tried to walk, but she couldn't. Each time, she fell back down. She was about seven years old and bone thin. I had the fleeting thought that this was not the well-fed child of a noble. She was so small. I lifted her up and with her legs wrapped around my waist, started to walk. Her head nestled on my chest, her breathing fast and shallow. Thalia picked up the sword from the ground and we started down the path. It didn't take long for her to get heavy, making us move awkwardly, but still we lumbered forward. Next to me, Thalia turned over her shoulder to look behind us, but there was nobody there.

My thighs burned from the added weight and I was out of breath. Then I saw it. Up ahead, the masts of Theseus' ship sliced through the night sky like a sword. Moonlight lit up the beach where the ship floated like a beacon. It was clear. No soldiers. We hobbled toward it when I again heard footsteps thumping up behind us. Unable to run, I planted my feet and turned. Next to me, Thalia held the sword. Theseus grinned back at me.

He was dirty and covered with blood, but relief crashed over me when I saw his face. "We defeated the archers, but there are more coming. We need to go." He lifted the girl from my chest like she was made of feathers.

"Sachi, what trouble did you get into?" he asked playfully. She giggled and buried her face in his chest.

I pointed at his ship.

"Yes. Go," he ordered.

"The men. What about the crew? Who will sail it?" Panic swelled. This was the part of the plan I hadn't thought about. In my mind, we would step on the ship and sail off, but this wasn't how it worked. Ships require a crew, oarsmen and a captain, none of which I'd considered. How could I be so dumb?

He raised his eyebrows and nudged my shoulder, amused at my stupidity. "Don't worry, Princess. My men will be there. Either way, they were to return back to Athens tonight. They will be ready."

Thalia didn't move. Darius burst from the brush, breathing heavy and covered with blood. Thalia threw herself into him, almost knocking him over. Frantic, she ran her hands over his arms and chest, over the cut on his face, searching for the source of the blood. Darius stilled her hand. "I'm all right. It's not my blood." Relieved, she rested her head on his chest.

Theseus held out his hand. "Come. We don't have much time. More guards will be coming."

My fingers closed around his and we ran together, with Sachi clinging around his neck, through the dark toward the ship. I hoped he was right and his men were ready. If not, we were stuck. His was not a big war ship. It was smaller, more the size of a royal transport, but there was no way the four of us and a bunch of children could even get it out of the harbor.

The descent to sea level was steep and rocky. In the

259

dark, I stumbled several times but kept going. I was thankful I wasn't carrying Sachi, but she didn't seem to slow Theseus down. Soon, we broke through the brush and stepped onto the sandy soil. His ship bobbed in the deeper water. There was a small boat with a single oar poised to ferry us over. We piled in the little boat and Darius rowed us over to the rope ladder.

It was shakier than I expected and I gripped each rung, working to keep it steady. I didn't want to start this journey by tumbling head over feet into the bay. When I planted both feet firm on the deck, I collapsed out of the way to make room for the others. True to his word, there were at least thirty men waiting on the oars below deck. The children sat quietly in the middle of the galley between the two rows of oarsmen. Up top, sailors were raising the black sail, black to blend into the darkness. Silently, I thanked the gods. Perhaps he was blessed by Poseidon, after all. I couldn't believe this was happening, that I was standing on a ship in the middle of the night. An Athenian ship.

With a quick kiss on her forehead, Theseus handed Sachi to me and darted into the captain's quarter. He came out with a hulking bronze club, the famous one he stole from the bandit. It was the weapon of a giant. I put a steadying hand on his arm. I didn't know what he was planning on doing, but the look on his face gave me chills. I wanted to get out of the harbor before soldiers flooded the beach.

He kissed me on the cheek. "They cannot follow us," was all he said before disappearing down the ladder. His silhouette jogging along the beach reminded me of Hercules, hulking and powerful. I watched with horror as he raised his club high and smashed the hull of one of my father's warships. I gasped and lurched forward to stop him, but Thalia stayed my hand.

"Ari, he's right. They cannot follow us."

Sachi buried her head in my neck and I held her close. Thalia clutched my shaking hand in hers as we watched him go down the line of ships, smashing each one until the whole fleet sagged, bobbing in an uneven tilt in the harbor. My father's prized ships lay ruined. What had I done?

When Theses returned, breathless, sweaty and glowing, the sailors drew up the anchor, lowered the rudders, readied the oars, and awaited the order to sail. He stomped twice on the deck and signaled to the sailors. Under our feet below deck, the Row Master called out the strokes.

"Ena." The oars dropped into the water with a unified splash.

"Dio." The oars cut into the water in unison. The boat lurched backward and pulled away from the harbor.

Smooth and light, we turned around in the harbor and paused there. All the oars went silent and we waited. The sailors on deck looked to Theseus. He nodded. At his command, four sailors with bows stepped forward, lit the tip of their arrows, aimed and fired them across my father's slumping fleet. One by one, the masts lit up, engulfing the night sky in an inferno of orange and yellow. Leaden gray smoke wafted from the ships, making the air a thick, silver haze. I heard the alarm sound on the shore, but didn't see any soldiers. I imagined my father springing out of bed, seeing the orange glow in the harbor, assembling his troops and watching our ship glide off into the darkness.

I wondered when he would realize the extent of my treason or even that I was gone, that I had fulfilled the awful prophecy. Leaving Crete under the shroud of smoke, we slid away. Shaking, I clutched an Athenian child while my father's ships burned.

My legs felt numb and shaky. I sunk to the floor, still holding Sachi on my lap. I couldn't watch. I couldn't speak. As of this moment, I was no longer a princess. I didn't see my island get smaller in the distance. I don't know the moment when it was no longer visible.

I stared at the stars until the tears came. I cried until I felt empty, tears for my family, my life that I could never return to, even Asterion, who I had wronged so horribly. Sachi rested her head on my chest and I smoothed her soft hair. Her shoulder had stopped bleeding. Darius and Thalia sat intertwined next to us.

We sat in silence, listening to the rhythmic slash of the oars in the water.

Out on the sea, the black of the water and the night sky swallowed everything except for a sprinkle of stars overhead. We didn't light lanterns because we didn't want to be seen and although we were relieved to be at sea, tension hung in the air. Sailors didn't normally sail at night because it was too dangerous. Stories of monsters with tentacles and gaping mouths of whirlpools circled through seaports, along with tales of beautiful maidens with sharp teeth that lured sailors to their deaths. Everyone knew someone who knew someone who narrowly escaped one of these creatures.

The crew was quiet and nervous, but they settled into a rhythm. Despite the dangers in the water, all of our lives depended on disappearing, so they kept rowing. The rest of us stayed out of the way. Theseus stood at the helm with his captain, their heads together deep in conversation. Occasionally, one pointed at the sky and the other nodded. Darius joined the rowers and Thalia and I huddled together on the deck at the front of the ship. Sachi curled herself into my lap. The heavy weight of her body and the steady rise and fall of her breath comforted me. With the rock of the ship, the slap of the waves and the safety of my lap, it didn't take long for her to fall asleep.

When we reached the open sea, I tried to stop

checking behind us. There was no pursuit. Theseus was thorough in smashing my father's ships and there would be none ready to chase us. Still, I kept staring into the black void. We were alone in the calm sea. The only sound was the splash of the oars slicing through the water and the rhythmic call of the row master. Minutes stretched into hours as Thalia and I sat wide awake, occupied by our own thoughts.

When I closed my eyes, I saw my father's ships ablaze and guards I had known my whole life shooting arrows at me. Over and over, my mind replayed our retreat, me running from my home, deserting my people, Asterion's severed head on the chest of the slain guard. It was a bad dream that I couldn't wake from. I felt lost and sick, but in my heart, I knew helping Theseus was the right thing to do. Thalia was safe. The children were safe. There would be no more people sacrificed to the labyrinth. I imagined my parent's reaction when they discovered what I'd done and I hoped that someday they would forgive me. I prayed to the gods that they wouldn't feel a need for vengeance and send a fleet to Athens. I hoped Theseus was right and our marriage would unite our two kingdoms.

Marriage.

That word sent fresh pangs of guilt through me. What would Phaedre do in the morning? She helped me save Thalia and I ran off, taking her dreams of being an Athenian queen with me. She would never forgive that betrayal. When I thought of Phaedre, feelings of hope and regret tumbled over each other. When I thought of my parents, I felt sick. Next to me, Thalia was still. I wondered what thoughts kept her awake. I rested my head on her shoulder and she squeezed my hand. At least, we had each other.

The oarsmen rowed for hours and by the time the top of the sun poked through the horizon, they needed a break. We all needed one. I was hungry and restless. My bottom was numb from sitting on the hard floor and my legs ached from being cramped underneath me. There wasn't much room to walk around on the ship and since movement and noise distracted the oarsmen, we all tried to be as still and quiet as possible. Now, we needed to stretch our legs and move around, especially the children who were getting wiggly. Even Sachi woke fidgeting in my lap. During the night, I redressed her shoulder once, but she fell back to sleep. She still hadn't spoken, but she seemed to be feeling better when she woke.

The captain, whose name I learned was Rastus, pointed at the red cliffs jutting out of the sea ahead and announced that this was where we would stop and rest. He was an older man with gray, curly hair, and a long nose. Despite his surprising soft voice, he made me nervous. Since I boarded the ship, he never acknowledged me and when he did look at me, his gaze was furtive and hard.

As we drifted into the bay, I watched the red cliffs

265

and sharp black rocks get closer. It looked so different from my island, sharp where Crete was smooth. Cliffs, but not the great mountain where Zeus was raised. There were no villages along the shoreline and I wondered where the people lived. Maybe on the other side of the island.

The crew hoisted the rudders and set down their oars. The anchor splashed into the turquoise water and we crammed together, eager to disembark. As the men scrambled into line, Theseus put a hand on Darius' chest.

"Wait," he said.

"Yes, sir?" Darius responded, unsure.

"Darius, thank you for your assistance on the beach as well as on the ship. You learned the oars quickly and I'm glad to have your strength."

Darius bowed. "Thank you, my lord."

"There is a problem though. You are a slave, are you not?"

Darius looked down. "Yes, sir."

"I'm a prince of Athens. I cannot sail a ship crewed by slaves. It would be a disgrace to the esteemed navy of Athens. I cannot arrive home carried by slaves."

Next to me, Thalia stiffened and Darius looked at the floor, almost resigned, as if waiting to hear he was going to be left behind. What Theseus said was true. Although slaves were common, the navy was a place for nobles and working men.

After an awkward moment of silence, Theseus

continued. "So, as of this moment, you are part of my galley and you are a free man. You will collect payment with the others when we arrive in Athens. My men will get you suitable clothes."

Thalia gasped. Darius looked stunned. He swept a deep bow. "Thank you, my lord. I will strive to honor you." Theseus nodded in return and turned to Thalia. "If you are to be my wife's maid and his wife, I wish you also to be free."

Thalia bowed before Theseus. "Thank you, my lord. I do not know what else to say."

He nodded at them and turned to me, his bright blue eyes tired, but clear. Dirty, sweaty and windblown, with dried blood on his tunic, he had never looked more attractive to me. I fought the urge to throw my arms around him. "Thank you," I said, smiling at him. He did what I couldn't. "You have given us all freedom."

He beamed back at me. "Princess, without you, I would still be in the labyrinth. You have given up much to help me. We have given each other freedom." He squeezed my hand. "I'm afraid this is not a proper port." He indicated the shoreline, where his men were rowdy, swimming in the shallow water and splashing with the children. "You will have to exit like my men, which is not fit for a princess."

"It's all right," I said. "I'm no longer a princess."

~ 19 ~

I jumped off the ladder and closed my eyes as my feet pierced the water like an arrow. The clear water washed over me, and cleaned off the dirt of the previous night, bringing me to life. I floated on my back in the arms of this unknown, wild harbor, weightless in the gentle sway of the waves, feeling the sun warm my face. For the first time, I felt free.

The crew emerged from the clear waters and sought out patches of shade beneath trees or next to rocks. Some sprawled out on the warm sand. After rowing all night, it didn't matter to them where they slept. Safe on the beach, they collapsed, Theseus included. He flopped down, leaned against a large rock on a shaded damp patch of sand, and watched his men make camp.

The children had energy to burn. Giggling, they splashed and chased each other around the beach. Sachi joined in as well, digging a hole in the sand with a little boy about her age. I watched her for a moment, amazed by her resilience. Her arm hung limp from her injured shoulder, but it didn't slow her down. Now that we were on land, we would need to take care of that shoulder, but for now, I was content to watch her play in the sand. With her hands in the water and dirt on her face, Sachi looked happy. I didn't relish the thought of causing her more pain. Thalia and I watched a castle emerge from the sand pile, and I thought back to how they looked last night, quiet and watchful. On this little island beach, they were children again. Regardless of what happened, that I had a part in creating their laughter made me happy.

A gnawing in my stomach reminded me that I should stop lolling on the beach. Not wanting to get in the way of the activity on the beach, Thalia and I decided to explore the island for food. Supplies on the ship were limited and dwindling. I also needed to find herbs for Sachi's shoulder. Before we left, the sailors filled the larder with a lot of wine and some bread and cheese, but not much else. We instructed the older children to look after the younger ones, and headed out past the beach.

Over the black boulders, we found a scraggly forest. Rock hard dirt and scrub gave way to taller trees, grasses and flowers. It was so similar to home, but unfamiliar. For the first time ever, I didn't know my way around. I didn't know the subtle flow of the land or where the fruit grew. It was thrilling, but a little unnerving. Tentative at first, we soon found our rhythm. Flowers grew everywhere and we picked them and wound them through our hair.

I plucked a round red fruit from a spindly bush popping up through the dry, cracked soil.

"Thalia," I said, holding it up. "What is this?"

She studied it and leaned in to sniff it. "I don't know. It smells sweet."

It smelled fresh and green and there was no milky sap. I went through a mental catalog of all the berries I knew from Crete and the knowledge gleaned from my mother. I knew of only one that was poisonous, the white berry of the nightshade. This fruit was definitely not nightshade and it looked and smelled sweet. "I think it's safe." I said and popped it in my mouth, hoping I was right that it wasn't poisonous. The burst of juicy sweetness made my mouth water. It tasted like a little tomato.

We plucked the bush clean of the red fruits and went in search of more, popping them in our mouths as we went along. To my delight, we found several small bushes and my cloak, which had become a makeshift basket, was getting full. We also found several patches of herbs, including bunches of chamomile, which would be useful steeped in water

270

to treat Sachi's shoulder and even the minor muscle aches of the crew. Soon, my cloak was heaped full of herbs, berries and edible plants. After everything the crew had done to help us get here, it felt good to be able to bring something back to share.

It felt right exploring with Thalia. I tried not to think of what happened or what the future held in Athens and focused instead on enjoying the adventure. Breathing in the clean, earthy smells of the forest unknotted the ball of guilt in my stomach. The sun burned through the thin clouds and parched the earth around us, sapping our energy. We couldn't find water anywhere. There were no springs or streams here. Finally, just outside a small cave at the base of a steep hill, we found a small spring. Relieved, we sat down and filled our water skins. Not realizing how thirsty I was, I gulped the cool, crisp water, enjoying the feeling of it traveling all the way to the bottom of my stomach. Overhead, birds cooed and insects buzzed. I was happy.

For the first time since we were children, we were just two girls enjoying a warm fall day together. Where we were quiet before, now the words spilled out in a flood. We talked about Darius and their new freedom and what our lives would be like in Athens. That turned into how we would arrange our houses and what food we would serve at their wedding and what they would name their children.

Still, I worried. The only things I knew of Athens

271

were the fanciful stories Alcina told me and our bleak history of war. I hoped King Aegeus would accept me. My fear deep down was that he would send me back to my father. What would I do then? I could not go home. That possibility burned along with my father's ships. Thalia reassured me that the king would welcome me as a princess of Crete and as his son's bride. I hoped she was right. How quickly things were changing. Only a few days ago, I was trying to sneak out of the weaving room. Our futures were uncertain. Today, we were collecting food on a strange island, both about to be married. It didn't seem real.

With my cloak full, I realized we needed to get back to the beach. The sailors would be waking up and we had a lot of food to share. On the way back, we retraced our steps so we wouldn't get lost. Around the area where we found the chamomile, I noticed something different. Among the few barren trees and tufts of brush, a single grapevine climbed up a shrub, its leaves spread wide to collect the sunlight.

For a moment, my heart froze. I ran up to the vine, sucking in a quick breath and covering my mouth. Dionysus. With my heart pounding, I spun around, trying to find him. There was nobody there. A second, closer look at the vine showed there were no grapes on it. It was just a lone, craggy vine, nothing more. Anything else was just wishful thinking. My shoulders slumped. There were no spontaneous grapes bursting from the earth. No little blue flowers to show me the path. I felt the makeshift basket, heavy with the food we gathered ourselves and looked over at Thalia next to me. It was enough, I decided. Whatever lay ahead, we could do this ourselves.

* * *

The beach was awake. A fire roared, poked at by a boy with a glowing stick, while a barrel-chested man looked on, cleaning fish. Sailors bustled around the beach, joking with each other as children played in the surf. Piles of fish waited to be prepared and makeshift shelters popped up among the rocks. They had been busy after their naps.

"Ariadne," Theseus said, coming toward me. All of the sailors stopped what they were doing to watch our approach. They were still wary of me. With a stab of panic, I squared my shoulders and held out the food we had gathered.

"We went out looking for food. I'm sorry that I didn't ask. You were all sleeping and- "

He stopped me. "You are not a prisoner here. You don't need to explain. I was worried, but I'm glad you're safe." He gave me an appraising look. Self-conscious, I tried to smooth my wild hair. After trekking through the woods for hours, I must have looked like a sweaty mess. I shifted on my feet and

273

picked at the dirt in my fingernails.

Theseus' eyes crinkled with a smile as he took both my hands. "Princess of Crete, I thank you for going in search of food. My men have caught some fish." Then, turning to his men, he boomed "We will have a feast tonight."

I flinched when he addressed me as princess. I'd thrown that title away with everything else I knew. At least he wasn't mad. I was prepared to fight, to explain myself like I usually did when I was caught sneaking out. Instead, he beamed at me. With nothing to see, the men turned back to their tasks. Thalia brushed my shoulder and headed to where Darius chased children on the beach. Theseus took my hand and led me to the fire, where I put down the bundle of food.

"You are a… surprise," he said. "I've never met a princess who would venture off into an unknown wilderness to search for food for a bunch of sailors."

I waved him off, shifted my eyes to the side. "I'm not a princess anymore."

"No," he said. "You are a warrior. A queen."

I laughed at his confidence. "Your father is king. If we marry, I would be a princess again." Right back where I started, I thought.

He pushed a stray hair out of my face and brushed his hand across my cheek. "Yes, but one day, you shall be a queen. My queen."

My skin woke up where he touched me. His gaze

rested on mine and I fell into those blue eyes that had seen so much of the world. Before I could drown in them, I broke our connection and looked at the beautiful black and red rocks of the island. I didn't want him to affect me this way. I was not Phaedre, won with pretty words and the promise of a title, but for the first time, I thought maybe it would be all right to be a queen. With a king like Theseus, it would certainly never be boring.

As the sky turned from orange to pink and purple, we feasted on the beach around a dancing fire, passing a wine skin and telling stories. The more the men passed the wine, the bigger their tales became. They chided each other over misadventures and roared over their victories.

Thalia and Darius cuddled up together, with Sachi dozing in Thalia's lap. After we returned, I mixed the herbs and Thalia pulled out the remaining arrow shaft. Lacking the time to make a proper poultice, I packed the wound with the herbs and we re-bandaged her shoulder. Now, she could heal. Sachi snuggled in and Thalia draped a protective arm over her. To anyone first seeing them, they would appear like a young family. I supposed they were.

Theseus and I leaned comfortably together against a large rock. I dug my toes into the cool sand, and pulled my cloak around me. I relaxed, sometimes asking questions about different places or people, but mainly just enjoying their adventures, happy the crew loosened up around me. A story about a young sailor who accidentally got tossed overboard trying to adjust the mast had me in peels of laughter, but the children only wanted to hear stories of Theseus making his way to Athens. The stories came alive as he told them.

"So, I spotted a small, bright house hidden in the trees and thought it would make a splendid place to spend the night," he started. "The owner, old Procrustes, welcomed me and told me of his magic bed. I was so tired and a magic bed sounded like a wondrous thing!" The children laughed. They knew this story and where it was going.

"Well, there was nothing magic about it. Everybody fits in his bed because if they were too tall, he cut their legs to make them shorter and if they were too short, he'd stretch them." At that last part, Theseus stood up and picked up a boy by the arms and pretended to stretch him. The boy laughed and squirmed.

"What was I going to do? I didn't want this crazy old man to cut off my legs! He led me to his magic bed and all the while, I'm thinking about how I'm going to get out of this and get back home. Then, he made a mistake. He turned his back on me." Here Theseus paused, the kids were spellbound.

"I stuck out my leg and tripped him as he walked past and put him into his own magic bed. Would you believe he was too tall for his own bed? Turns out, the bed was magic after all because when I got him tucked in, he fit perfectly."

The kids were in love, laughing at the stupidity of old Procrustes. Thalia shot me a look because the version she heard in the marketplace was much bloodier. Still, I watched him telling the story, with the glow from the fire bouncing off his face and I found I didn't care.

One after another, the children requested more stories and he told them all. They howled with laughter, especially when he told them of bending down the pine tree and flinging the Pine Bender into the air.

When he tired of telling stories, his men took over and Theseus sat back down at my side. With my belly full, the warm fire and the hour growing late, my eyes grew heavy. Theseus gently slipped his arm around my back and I rested my head on his shoulder. He smelled of salt-water and smoke. As I relaxed into him, Thalia's eyes bore into me, but I ignored her. I drifted to sleep under the black sky, feeling safe and content. The last thing I remember was a soft kiss on my forehead as he pulled me in closer.

* * *

The morning sky was a riot of yellow and orange, the hot sun washing the beach in warmth. It was a new day. I woke with my head on Theseus' chest and stayed for a while listening to the steady rhythm of his heartbeat as I watched a seagull poke at scraps from last night's feast. I was the first one awake. Drowsy and content, I wanted to spend the entire day here between worlds, watching this bird, but I knew I couldn't. We needed to set sail.

We needed to get to Athens. The longer we waited, the more time my father had to rebuild his fleet. Out here, if my father sought revenge, it would be easy. We were a bare crew of sailors and children. Without the support of Athens' fleet, we weren't a match for my father's navy. I searched the horizon for the tall masts of Crete's warships, but it was empty.

By now, my father would have noticed I was gone. Would he think I was kidnapped and taken by force? Did he know the extent of my betrayal of Crete? He knew who captained the ship and where we were heading. We were one ship. He wouldn't need more than that to intercept us. Since he hadn't, the truth prickled at me. He didn't come for me.

Did I want to see sails on the horizon? I got up and walked to the edge of the foamy surf, letting the cold water lap at my feet and thought about this. I didn't want to go back to Crete. This I knew. But, selfishly perhaps, I wanted to be missed. I wanted them to see me, to see my value outside of my marriage prospects. More than anything, I wanted them to understand why I did it and why I couldn't stay. I hoped Phaedre didn't hate me. At one time, my mother also felt this pull to be something more.

278

Perhaps in time, she would understand.

I sat down on the ground and resting my head on my knees, traced circles in the gritty black sand. Before long, the sailors woke and as they shook off sleep, the beach came to life. Men tumbled into action gathering supplies and getting the ship ready, while the children trailed behind them trying to help. Thalia came over to sit next to me, her face radiant, happy. She bumped my shoulder and suggested that perhaps we could assist by getting some more food. I didn't want to look at the horizon anymore and she was right. We had a few hours before the ship would be ready to sail. She pulled me to my feet and we headed back into the forest.

In the grove, that one withered grapevine now hung heavy with grapes. Overnight, it had spread out, winding among the shrubs. I ran my hands along the large, smooth leaves and silently thanked the God of Wine for watching out for us. Although, I knew I wouldn't find him, I couldn't help but search for him in the shadows of the forest. Every time a branch rustled, I turned around hoping to see him.

"You'll see him again," Thalia said, throwing an arm around my shoulder.

"I know."

After collecting all the fruit, we explored a new area, where we found asparagus, some beans and little tomatoes. Satisfied with our haul, we stopped at the spring to fill our water skins and lounged by the cave before heading back to the beach.

By the time I got back, the ship was almost ready. A young sailor took our food, thanked us heartily and rushed off to add it to the larder on the ship. Theseus seemed distracted, making sure his crew stayed on task, but when he saw me, he brightened and came over, folding me in his arms. Strong and solid, he smelled of salty air and smoke from the fire. What appeared to me like a bright, breezy day worried some of the sailors. The seas around the islands are known to get rough this time of year and they studied the waves with trepidation. With a slight smile, Theseus warned me not to eat anything yet.

The sailors boarded the ship first, with the children scrambling behind them. Before settling in to my place on the floor at the helm, I walked to the back of the ship and looked out over the wide sea. It seemed limitless, like the holder of buried secrets. I moved to the front for a last glance at the island and then settled into my spot next to Thalia. At the head, Theseus conferred with the captain and signaled his men. The row master called out the stroke and the ship lurched forward. A lilting melody from a flute synced the oars and the notes draped over us like a comfortable blanket. As the ship rocked, I listened to the crash of the oars in the water, drawing us to my new life.

After several hours of sailing, I noticed that the seagulls had stopped swooping around us. Billowy white clouds floated overhead in the blue sky, but no birds. At the helm, Theseus glanced at the sky repeatedly, raking his hand over his head, worried. The wind kicked up. We were crammed together in the ship, the sailors sweaty and practically on top of each other. At times, the smell was stifling. The cool wind rushing through felt like a welcome bath. Then, the waves grew, smashing against the sides of the ship, throwing it back and forth. Ours was not a giant warship, heavy with men and artillery. It was smaller and the sea easily tossed it around.

Waves crashed, sending shards of white spray over the edge. The ship lurched and jerked, as the sea made sport with it. At times, it felt like we floated on our side before another wave slammed us back down. Someone screamed. Positioned in the middle of the rowers, the children couldn't see much, but the violence of the shifts scared them. The smaller ones started to cry, while the older ones held them, frozen with fear. Some got sick. Still, the sailors kept rowing, kept trying to stay the course.

The sea threw us around, up and down and back and forth. Hot chills crept up my back to the top of my head and settled in my stomach, making me glad I hadn't eaten. Next to me, Thalia trembled and gripped my arm. We clung together as the sea roiled beneath us. I closed my eyes, trying to center myself, to find the rhythm. Even when they're rough, waves flow in a pattern. Like my feet in the labyrinth, I tried to find order in the chaos of the waves.

BRRRAFFF! The sea roared as a big wave ripped through, lifting the ship and slamming it back down. We clutched on to each other and whatever seemed stable to keep ourselves from being thrown. Even in the pauses between waves, everything shook. White foam soaked the deck as white-tipped waves beat the wooden frame. Still we kept on, fighting our way over the waves and through the sea.

When the high mountains on the island of Naxos came into view, the crew cheered. I barely saw it. My head pounded and I was so dizzy I couldn't focus my eyes. The last thing I remember was the crack of wood being torn apart and then darkness.

~ 20 ~

When I opened my eyes, all I saw was purple sky. It reminded me of a bruise. My feet dangled and bounced and my head throbbed. Through a fog, I realized I was being carried. I murmured something unintelligible into Theseus' neck and he shushed me before gently setting me down in the soft sand. I gripped the grainy sand in my fists to stop the ground from spinning. Theseus frowned down at me, concerned. I could tell he was talking, but I couldn't hear what he was saying. The ringing in my ears was overpowering. I was so tired. If I could only close my eyes for a few minutes.

The next thing I knew, it was dark. My head

throbbed and the ringing in my ears had quieted to a dull squeal. I still felt the roll of the ship, though I was firmly in the sand with Thalia asleep next to me, our arms intertwined. My head rested on someone's lap. For a moment, I thought it was Dionysus, but when I raised my head, it was Theseus with his arm around my waist. Blinking back the confusion, I nudged myself to sit.

"There she is. Welcome back," he said.

"What happened?" I asked, sitting up and rubbing the back of my head, where a bump had sprung up and was now radiating pain.

"We made it to Naxos."

"Naxos?" I slumped back down against him.

"One of the supports on the mast broke off and hit you on the head." He motioned over to Thalia, still sound asleep next to me. "If it hadn't been for her, you would have gone over the side. She grabbed you and wouldn't let go."

Oh, Thalia, thank you.

"My head hurts." It was all I could think to say.

"I bet. Don't worry. You'll be fine. Just rest."

"Where are all the people?" I said, looking around the deserted beach. If we made it to Naxos, where were the villages? Where was everybody?

He tilted his head and gave me a quizzical look, trying to understand what I was asking. "Oh, most of the villages are farther east. There are some on this end, but we docked on the part of the shore without a port. With the mast broken, we didn't have much choice and even if we did, we don't want to draw attention."

He didn't know, I thought. He didn't know that my father wasn't coming for me. My brain felt thick and slow, like trying to run through deep water. I picked up my head to tell him and pain screamed through my skull and down the back of my spine. Theseus smiled down on me.

"It's all right," he said. "We'll talk later. Just rest."

Groups of people lied clustered together in the sand. Safe. In front of me, the last flames of the fire simmered, the embers glowing orange. The smell of fish lingered in the air, making my stomach curdle. I leaned back into Theseus, resting my heavy head back on his shoulder and closed my eyes.

I awoke to a feeling in my stomach I couldn't ignore. Theseus was gone and I was alone. I sat up just in time for the meager contents of my stomach to come spilling out. Over and over, I heaved until I was empty. The pain in my head had dulled to a low hum and I rested my face on the cool, damp sand. I heard the patter of footsteps on the sand and squinted up to Thalia kneeling beside me, her face full of concern. She pulled me up to standing and handed me a skin of water.

"Drink," she said. "You'll feel better."

I drank. The fresh water spread its fingers through my belly, restoring me. I took a deep breath and blinked, trying to focus my eyes. She buried the mess I made and pulled me up. On shaky legs, I stumbled a little further down in the sand, which felt solid and comforting. Morning sunshine bounced off the water, making the surface glisten. Unlike the first island, with its black, rocky, craggy beaches, the golden shoreline on Naxos stretched out for miles. Thalia and I sat together in silence for a few moments.

"When we dreamed of going on adventures on a ship, I don't think that's what we pictured," she said with a little smile.

"I couldn't have imagined that," I agreed. "Theseus said that you saved me. Thank you."

She put her arm around me. "Always."

I smiled back at her and sipped my water.

"Is everyone all right?" I asked, suddenly remembering the terror of the children huddled together.

She nodded. "Yes. Shaken up, but all right. A lot of the children were sick, but they recovered quickly. They do. The sailors are fine. They aren't strangers to the sea."

"Thank goodness. So… what happens now?"

"Theseus said that we need to fix the mast. Some have gone to the village seeking wood."

"How far is the village?"

"They said they had to go inland and would be gone for several hours."

She looked over at me, creases of concern furrowing

her brow. "I'm all right," I said. "Don't worry. Just a little sore."

She didn't seem convinced, but left it alone. "They were able to save most of the food. Some of it got wet, but not all. There's still some bread. I put some aside for you so nobody else would eat it." She brought a chunk of bread out of her bag and set it on my lap.

"When you're ready."

"The last of the bread from home," I said, smiling. "Thank you. I will enjoy it."

Satisfied that I was more or less all right, Thalia left me alone so she could tend to the children. I nibbled my breakfast and watched her on the beach, ruffling hair and giving hugs. Darius joined her and the children crowded around, jostling for position. He tossed one of the little boys in the air, caught him and swept him back into the air. Thalia was always strong and capable, but on the beach surrounded by children and Darius at her side, she looked happy.

I spent the morning in the spot where she left me, fading in and out of sleep, enjoying the warmth of the sunshine. My head still swam, and my stomach felt hollow and raw, but I didn't get sick again. Despite having no energy, the feeling that I should be doing something nagged at me, but there didn't seem to be anything for me to do. The men worked on the ship. Thalia and Darius went into the woods searching for food and water. So, I sat on the beach watching the children splash around. I sipped my water, which I

287

now noticed contained a sprig of mint. Out in the deeper waters, dolphins played. I loved watching them shoot out of the sea in a playful arc.

After a while, I started to feel more like myself and I got bored and restless. I scanned the beach for Theseus, but I didn't see him. I still felt a little unsteady, and I wanted someone to know where I was going. I called out to one of the sailors that I was going for a walk and after he waved, I shuffled off through the low brush. I didn't want to go too far. Beyond the beach, the golden sand continued in rolling waves with clumps of wildflowers and tufts of thorny bushes poking their heads out. Beyond that, a forest of cedar trees spread inward. I suspected that was where Thalia and Darius went.

I poked around the clearing, picking some wildflowers and bunches of thyme, which smelled clean and earthy. I stopped beneath an old olive tree on a hill to take a rest when I heard voices. Not knowing who it was, I ducked out of sight down the slope, behind the tree.

"You can't marry her."

"What do you mean?"

"Your father won't have it."

"I gave her my word. Besides, without her help, I wouldn't have gotten out."

With a start, I recognized the voice of Theseus and his captain, Rastus. I crouched lower, pressing myself into the side of the hill. Trying to keep still, my heart thumped. They were almost across from me. I crouched down lower, hoping I was far enough down that they wouldn't see me if they turned this way.

"It doesn't matter. Her father waged this war. Took our sons, even our daughters. She will not be welcomed as a bride."

"No. She helped saved them."

"That's not how the people will see it."

Theseus sighed. "They can be made to see."

Rastus continued, "You left Athens a warrior. You need to return a warrior. You slew the beast. You saved Athens. That is how you need to return. Not as some lovesick boy with a pretty girl."

Theseus said something that I couldn't hear, followed by a long pause.

"What am I supposed to do with her? She can't go back." Theseus sounded annoyed, his voice slipping into a childish whine.

"You can bring her back to Athens, just not as your bride."

"As what then?" Theseus paused and then continued, "Oh," as he realized what Rastus was saying. "My prize."

The word hit like an punch to my stomach.

Rage welled up inside me. How dare they talk about me this way? I gave up everything to help him. They think he's going to take me back to Athens as a prize of war? As bounty he'd won? A whore to be paraded through town, defeated like a spoil of war? No. That was not happening.

I sat shaking with rage waiting for Theseus and Rastus to leave. They stood together, deep in conversation, but I couldn't hear what they said. Finally, they left and I listened to their footsteps receding down the path. For several moments, I sat in shock. My head ached and swam. I paced back and forth, cursing them, trying to collect my thoughts and see the way forward.

I couldn't let him take me back to Athens like that. Could I change his mind? I shook my head. No, it was doubtful. What Rastus said was probably true. It was foolish to think we could unite our countries when there was so much anger between them. They would only see me as the daughter of their enemy. I couldn't go to Athens. But, where would I go? What would I do?

One step at a time. I needed to figure out how to get Theseus to leave me behind. If I told him I'd overheard his conversation, he would deny it. Could I run away? No. If I did that, he would look for me. Or Thalia would. She couldn't do that. If I had to go back to Crete, she couldn't come with me. With my parents, she would always be in danger. No. Thalia was free now and she needed to go have her life with Darius. I owed her that. Theseus would keep his word to her. There was no political gain for him not to. This was something I needed to do myself.

I trudged back to the beach, angry and hurt. When I

saw the crash of the waves on the shore, clarity hit me like a broken mast to the head. I knew what I had to do.

~ 21 ~

I slipped back into camp and flopped down on the blanket in the sand where I had spent the night. I didn't talk to anybody for the rest of the afternoon. When people came to check on me, I pretended to be asleep. Now, as I lie there, staring up at the sky, my mind reeled. The horizon was on fire, the bright orange evening sky eating through the soft afternoon blue. Wispy pink clouds stretched and pulled, nudged on their way by a gentle breeze. It was so beautiful, the transition from light to dark. The sadness inside of me hardened like a rock.

Thalia came and sat down beside me. I knew it was her without looking. Her fingers lightly trailed over the bump on my head, checking to see if it was bigger.

She seemed satisfied that it hadn't grown. I sat up and looked around, making sure nobody was near, and pulled her closer. She leaned in and I told her what I overheard, spitting out the word "spoil" like it was venom on my tongue. She was shocked, speechless. We sat next to each other in silence, looking out over the sea.

"I thought he loved you," she said after a while.

"He loves himself, but I was starting to think that maybe…"

"That coward!" she said. "I'll kill him."

I grabbed her hand, loving her for wanting to protect me.

"As much as I'd love to see that," I chuckled, "that's not the answer."

She cut me off. "Well, what are we going to do?"

"He has to leave me behind."

"No, you can't stay here by yourself."

"I have to. I can't go with him like that. I can't go home. I have to stay. Figure something out."

Resolve set on her face. "OK. I'll stay with you."

I squeezed her hand and stared at her. "No. You can't. You have to go. You can have a good life in Athens. Darius will have a job with Theseus."

Her eyes narrowed. "How could he? Knowing what he wants to do?"

"Even so, he'll be good to you. I believe that. He has honor."

"How do you know that? How do you know we

won't be part of his spoils too?"

"Because it wouldn't gain him anything. For a parade, he needs a noble. A princess of his enemy to put on display. He will keep his word with Darius."

She furrowed her brow, skeptical, but didn't argue the point. "So, what is your plan?"

"I will be too sick to voyage. I'll convince him to leave me here and get help in Athens and then come back for me."

"Come back?"

"I know what I heard, but I don't think that what passed between us was a lie. He seemed a little reluctant about bringing me back in chains. Perhaps, he just needs a way out. If so, maybe if he goes ahead, he can convince his father to bring me to Athens as his bride. If not, I suspect he won't come back at all. He will have other things to do."

"What if he doesn't?"

"There are villages and ships here. Friends of my father's. If he doesn't return, I will get one of them to take me back to Crete and throw myself at my father's feet."

Her eyes widened as she turned this over in her mind. "It is a risk. He'll be furious."

"Yes."

I laid back down and Thalia got a wet cloth for my forehead. For the rest of the night, I didn't leave my blanket and played the part of someone too sick to move. While everyone else ate, I stayed away, curled up on my blanket.

Theseus came over to check on me, bringing the last of the grapes. I could hear the crew by the fire, laughing and singing songs, but he seemed troubled and distracted. Thalia fussed over me, expressing concern over the growing bump on my head and I played into it, saying I felt weak and dizzy. We sat together, not speaking, with me leaning against him as he stroked my hair. I searched his face, looking for the tenderness from the days prior. It was there, along with something else, a hardness that wasn't present yesterday.

When he left to rejoin his men at the fire, he kissed my forehead and bade Thalia to take good care of me. He didn't meet my eyes. I needed to be strong for the voyage "home" in the morning. There were no niceties about meeting his father or what we would do in Athens, only concern that I was able to make the journey. Whatever hesitation I felt at my spotty plan evaporated. Despite anything he may feel for me, he was a prince of Athens first. He would do his duty.

Thalia slept next to me, sharing my blanket in the sand. We were quiet, both of us thinking of what needed to happen. I listened to the steady rise and fall of her breaths and eventually, I dropped off to sleep.

When I awoke, the beach was bustling with activity. Sailors tore down the camp and loaded the ship, getting ready to sail. Theseus came over to check on me and to make sure I was up. Thalia helped me to my feet and once I was upright, I turned and threw up into the brush behind me. I bent over, retching while Thalia rubbed my back and explained to Theseus that my condition was worse. To my surprise, it was easy to throw up on demand. My stomach was still a little queasy and his presence made it worse. Thalia explained the obvious about how I was still dizzy and my stomach unsettled. She feared for me making the journey and didn't think I could handle it. To prove her point, I collapsed back down on the ground, making a show of trying to get back up.

Eyes wide with concern, he took my face in his ends, studying me. I wanted to look away, but I held his gaze. My heart pounded. After a few moments, he said that I must go. We couldn't linger here and the doctors at Athens would treat me.

Desperate, I grabbed both his hands and started to cry. "Please," I begged "My head is screaming. I'm dizzy and I can't keep anything in my stomach. I can't go on the ship. I can't meet your father like this, weak and sick. I want to be strong, the princess Athens deserves. Athens isn't far. Go home. Fix the mast properly. Get a healer and return for me. In a few days, I will be ready to return with you."

He smoothed my hair and cupped my cheek and said, "I can't leave you here. What will you do?"

"I will be fine. Leave me some food and jugs of water. All I want to do is lie on the sand and rest.

You've built shelters all along the beach. Please."

"Well, it's true. Sailing like this will make it worse." He searched my face, considering the options. "Thalia can stay with you."

"No," I said. "The children need her. You have one more stop before Athens. They're restless, anxious to get home. You'll need her to keep them out of your way. I will be fine. I can take care of myself. Like you said, I need to rest and it will only be a few days." He knew this was true. Now, the children depended on Thalia. He had other duties and his men were not caretakers.

"One of my men then."

"No. There's no need. I just need to rest. I can do that well enough on my own."

He narrowed his eyes, unsure.

"Plus," I continued, taking his hand. "This will give you time to talk to your father and get his blessing."

His face brightened. "I have no doubt we will have his blessing, but you're right. It may be better not to surprise him. Then, I can come back and give you the welcome you deserve."

I sighed in relief. "Yes. I will be fine. I was raised on an island, you know." I managed a weak smile. I didn't add that I was raised in a palace and not a beach.

"All right. We will do as you suggest. As soon as we land, I will talk to my father and return for you."

He kissed my forehead and went back to supervise

the readying of the ship. I watched him walk away, feeling both relieved that he agreed to my plan and sadness that he would leave me here. I wished I would have learned how to build a fire. It would be all right, I assured myself. I can always walk to the village and find help. Thalia wouldn't look at me. She got to work gathering the rest of the bread, along with some of the meat from last night's dinner, a supply of water and a large mound of food she found in the woods. Piling it all up in front of me seemed to comfort her, but I didn't want to eat any of it. My stomach clenched in a knot of worry. Between the food and the shelters on the beach, it would be enough, I told her. I would be fine. I repeated it to both of us like a mantra.

Theseus came over multiple times to check on me and clear his conscience. Each time, he fidgeted, giving me repeated instructions on how to care for myself. He built a fire and left a pile of wood next to it. He was worried, but he didn't change his mind. Now, I grabbed his hand as he started to walk away.

"Promise me. Promise me that you will take care of Thalia and Darius."

He squeezed my hand. "I will. They are free. Darius will have a place in my guard. I swear it on the crown I gave you when we met."

The crown. It seemed like ages ago that he sprang up out of the water holding it in his hand. His brow furrowed in concern and I believed he would do what he promised. Whatever else happened, I knew he would keep them safe.

At last, the ship was ready and everyone started to board. Thalia crushed me to her, crying into my hair and telling me to take care of myself. We promised to see each other soon. Darius helped her on board and they waved to me from the side of the ship. He would protect her. No, they will protect each other. I will see them again, I told myself over and over.

I flopped down on the deserted beach, my heart heavy as I watched the oars slice the water and pull the ship into the sea. The black sails got smaller and smaller on the horizon and soon, I couldn't see them anymore. I sat on the beach until my legs cramped and my bottom got sore. Aside from the crackle of the fire next to me and the call of the gulls, the beach was quiet. For the first time in my life, I was entirely by myself. Even when I snuck off to the market, I was near the palace or close to people loyal to my father. There was always someone nearby. Now, I was truly alone. The only people who knew where I was were on that ship to Athens.

I thought of Thalia and Darius and little Sachi and sadness took my breath away. Tears ran down my face. I let them come. I thought about my home nestled in the mountains. How I knew every valley and hill. Alcina. She must be going crazy with worry. I looked at the pile of food in front of me, but it only made me miss the cook's honey cakes that I'll never have again. I cried for the life I lost. My family. I thought of my beautiful mother, who invented errands I could do in the woods and of my father, proud and willing to do whatever it took to keep his kingdom safe. Phaedre, so eager to rule, was the heir now and I hoped she was ready for it. Tears ripped through me. All the sadness I pushed down for my whole life poured out of me. The loneliness I felt at being different and the bond I felt with Asterion, the horrible beast, who listened to my stories and liked it when I brought bunches of lavender. I saw his bloody head resting on the stomach of the guard, that guard who wouldn't see his family again. Because of me. If Theseus didn't return, I couldn't go home. I had no home. My father didn't come for me. He didn't want me back. I'd lost everything. I sobbed and the pain flowed through me like water.

After a while, I had no more tears to cry. My eyes burned and my throat was raw. My breathing uneven. I picked myself up, brushed off the sand and looked out over the horizon. This life was my own and I needed to figure out what to do with it. Where to go. The waves lapped the shore and in the distance, a dolphin leaped out of the water. On the shore, seagulls circled searching for food. Life continued around me.

Music startled me out of my thoughts. Airy notes whispered from a lute floated through the breeze around me. I spun around checking for the source of the music, but I didn't see anything. Then, his dark head appeared over the outcropping of rocks.

"Princess," he said, arms outstretched, coming to stand before me. His amber eyes rested comfortably on me. "Why so sad?"

Dionysus. I looked at him in disbelief. "I've lost everything."

"Lost? You've gained what you most wanted. You're free."

"Free?"

"What happens now is up to you. Not your father. Not Athens. It's your life. To do with as you please."

I looked around at the golden beach with the sparkling waves, the high cliffs and the wispy clouds overhead. I glanced down at my dress, plain before but now dirty and torn. My hair had fought its way out of the ribbon. I took out the ribbon and let it blow free in the breeze.

"What are you doing here?" I asked.

"Isn't it obvious? I came for you."

"Me? I'm not one of your followers."

He chuckled. "No, you are definitely not a priestess. I want you by my side. As my wife."

"Your wife?" I repeated.

"I've wandered every country trying to gain the approval of my father. I've been rootless and lost. When I came upon you on the beach and you said my name, it felt like home. Come with me." He held his hands out to me.

I studied his face, that smile that crinkled his deep amber eyes, the way his eyebrows furrowed when he was being earnest. There were a million reasons to run the other way. Musicians sing countless stories of maidens who were loved and left by the gods. It always ends badly. Still, when I looked at him, I felt safe.

I took a step toward him and his hand brushed against my cheek, settling on the back of my neck. I studied his face, more like a man than a god. The corner of his mouth lifted into a smile. I drew my hand across his cheek, rough and worn. Our faces were close enough to share a breath, but I couldn't breathe. His lips brushed mine, softly at first and then with hunger. Warmth shot through me, waking up my entire body. We pulled apart and I pushed the wayward hair out of his face. My hand trailed down his neck and over his chest and slipped inside his tunic to rest on his heart. Under my hand, it thumped, matching the quick rhythm of my own. It wasn't the heart of a god. It was the heart of a man.

He put his hand on top of mine and brought it to his lips, giving it a quick kiss. As he led me down the path, he glanced back over his shoulder, his expression a boyish look of love and mischief. At that moment, I knew I was lost. Perhaps, also found.

"Come. There is much to see. Where do you want to go first?"

~ The End ~

Epilogue

I married him a few months later during the winter solstice. I wore a pale blue shimmery gown my mother would have loved. It moved like water and looked like the stars. On my head, I wore a wreath of red roses and I had only one attendant, Thalia. Dionysus surprised me by replacing my crown of roses with the crown Theseus pulled out of the sea on Crete. I didn't ask how he got it. Forged in the sea, fitted with the jewels of my island, he said it was destined to be mine. It was a simple ceremony, needing nobody's approval.

What happened afterwords, is a story for another day.

Author's Note

This book started with a question. I've always loved mythology and the stories that are passed on through the generations. The one about Theseus slaying the Minotaur always bothered me because I felt that the princess who helped him got overlooked. She seemed to risk everything to help him, but the way I'd always heard the story, she was just a silly, lovesick girl, used and abandoned on a beach. It seemed incomplete to me. I wondered why a princess would betray her family and her kingdom. She needed a voice. The other curious thing about Ariadne's story is that in mythology, where nearly every marriage is fraught with lies and disaster, her marriage seemed to be a happy one.

It's amazing where a little curiosity will take you.

Those two questions led to others and from that, I built her story. Along the way, I read many books on Cretan bronze age history and went down the Internet rabbit hole trying to piece together what her life might have been like. The truth is that we don't know. The writing from the Minoan time, with the exception of Linear B, is untranslated. That leaves us with the scenes painted on pottery and on frescoes in the elaborate buildings they left behind. They show an advanced society, rich in trade and artwork with a culture that was all their own and different from that of ancient Greece. I tried to use all of that, and my imagination, to flesh out Ariadne's world. Although they worshiped other gods, I used the Greek gods and goddesses because they are the most recognizable. Any historical errors are my own and I ask your forgiveness for those.

I'm so thankful for my husband, Chris, and my two boys and their unending love and support. Thank you to Ashley Rich for her editorial insight and for being kind and harsh when I needed it. My writing is better for it. I also need to thank my early readers, whose feedback is invaluable.

Most of all, thank you for spending time with my book. It means the world to me. I hope you enjoyed Ariadne's story.

Thank You

Thank you! I hope you enjoyed Ariadne's Crown. I had so much fun researching and writing it. Please take a moment to leave a review on Amazon, Goodreads or wherever you purchased the book. As an independent author, your reviews mean so much.

If you would like to be contacted when I release something new, please subscribe to my newsletter. I promise, I won't fill your inbox with nonsense and spam.

You can find the link to join, on my website – www.meadoehora.com.

About the Author

Meadoe Hora is the author of the Superhero Kick Team children's book series, which she wrote with her son, Bennet. This is her first full length novel. She lives in the Milwaukee, Wisconsin area with her husband, her boys, a spoiled basset hound, and a crazy black lab.

Websites:
www.meadoehora.com
www.meadooutonalimb.com

Social Media:
Instagram: meadoeoutonalimb
Facebook: meadoehorawrites
Snapchat:meadoehora19

Made in the USA
Monee, IL
18 June 2023